PADDINGTON
RACES AHEAD

by MICHAEL BOND

illustrated by R.W. ALLEY

HarperCollins *Children's Books*

First published in hardback in Great Britain by
HarperCollins *Children's Books* in 2012
First published in paperback in 2013

1 3 5 7 9 10 8 6 4 2

HarperCollins *Children's Books* is a division of
HarperCollins *Publishers* Ltd, 77–85 Fulham Palace Road,
Hammersmith, London W6 8JB.

Visit our website at
www.harpercollins.co.uk

ISBN: 978-0-00-745885-1

CONTENTS

Chapter One

MR CURRY'S BIRTHDAY TREAT

EARLY ONE SPRING morning Paddington hurried into the garden as soon as he had finished breakfast in order to inspect his rockery. He was an optimistic bear at heart, and having planted some seeds the day before, he was looking forward to seeing the results.

The seeds had been a free gift in one of Mrs

Brown's magazines, and the picture on the side of the packet was a blaze of bright yellow flowers. Some of them were almost as tall as the magazine's gardening expert, Alf Greenways.

Mr Greenways was known to his many friends in the trade as 'Beanpole Greenways', so it was as good a recommendation for success as anyone could possibly wish for.

He also owned the nursery supplying the sunflower seeds, so it was no wonder he was beaming all over his face as he held a watering can aloft, spurring his blooms to even greater heights.

Paddington got down on all fours and peered at the freshly-raked soil in his patch of garden, but apart from a disconsolate-looking caterpillar, there wasn't so much as the tiniest of green shoots to be seen. Everything was exactly as he had left it the night before when he had gone outside with a torch before going to bed.

Mr Greenway's seeds were rather large and he couldn't help wondering if he had planted them upside down by mistake.

A robin redbreast landed on a nearby rock to

take a closer look at what was going on, but having spotted Paddington's network of cotton threads protecting the patch, it flew off in disgust.

Mr Brown was right. Gardens were a good example of life in the raw; a constant battle between good and evil. Slugs, for example, were given very short shrift, often ending up with the contents of a salt cellar upended over them, whereas worms were always welcome – unless of course they happened to come up for air in the middle of the lawn.

All the same, it was disappointing, and for a moment or two Paddington toyed with the idea of going indoors and fetching his binoculars in case the caterpillar had a hearty appetite and he could see traces of green on its lips.

He was in the middle of weighing up the pros and cons when he heard an all-too-familiar voice calling out to him.

His heart sank as he looked up and saw the Browns' neighbour peering at him over the top of the fence. Not that there was anything new in that; Mr Curry was a notorious busybody and he spent his life poking his nose into other people's affairs.

Because his patch of garden coincided with some higher ground on Mr Curry's side, Paddington often bore the brunt.

It was most disappointing. Mr Brown had spent half of the weekend raising the fence at that particular point, with the express intention of putting a stop to their neighbour's spying.

At the time Mrs Bird had said 'the chance would be a fine thing' and it looked as though her worst fears were being realised.

"What are you doing, bear?" growled Mr Curry suspiciously. "Up to no good as usual, I suppose."

"Oh, no, Mr Curry," said Paddington. "I was just checking my blooms – except I haven't got any yet. Mrs Bird was right. She said you would be bound to find a box to stand on. I mean…"

"What was that, bear?" barked Mr Curry.

"Mrs Bird saw a fox in our garden the other day," said Paddington hastily. "She thinks it came over here because it couldn't find anything interesting in yours."

Paddington was normally the most truthful of bears and he stayed where he was for a moment or two in case the proverbial thunderbolt landed on his head, but nothing happened, so he breathed a sigh of relief and carried on looking for new plant shoots.

"I don't see any point in having flowers," growled Mr Curry. "Nasty things. They make the place untidy – dropping their petals everywhere. Just you wait."

"I was hoping Mr Brown might take a photograph of mine when they are ready," explained Paddington. "It's my Aunt Lucy's birthday in August and she says flowers always brighten things up. They don't have many in the Home for Retired Bears in Lima and I thought I could send her a picture she can keep by her bed."

A gleam entered Mr Curry's eyes and he suddenly perked up. "Do you know what day it is today, bear?" he asked casually.

Paddington thought for a moment. "I think it's a Wednesday, Mr Curry," he said.

"Nothing else about it?" asked Mr Curry.

"Not that I know of," said Paddington. "I can ask Mrs Bird if you like."

"I don't think that will be necessary," said Mr Curry hastily. Reaching inside his jacket pocket, he removed a folded sheet of paper.

"It's funny you should mention the word 'birthday', bear," he continued, waving it in the air. "Quite a coincidence, in fact. Don't tell anyone else, but it happens to be my birthday today."

"Does it really, Mr Curry?" exclaimed Paddington. "I didn't know that."

"Well," said the Browns' neighbour, "you do now, but since you have clearly forgotten the fact, it's…"

He broke off as the paper slipped from his fingers and they both watched it flutter to the ground on Paddington's side of the fence and land at his feet.

"Now look what you've made me do!" he barked. "I've dropped my list of presents… I sat up late last night making it out…"

Paddington looked shocked. "You haven't opened them already have you, Mr Curry?" he exclaimed. "Mrs Bird says that's supposed to be very unlucky."

"I don't have any to open yet, bear," said Mr Curry. "That paper you made me drop contains a

list of all the things I wouldn't mind having.

"I made it out in case anyone happens to be stuck for ideas," he added casually.

Paddington made haste to retrieve the paper. From a quick glance, it seemed to be rather long.

"Don't bother reading it now, bear," said Mr Curry hastily. "You can keep it to browse over at your leisure. However, there isn't much time left, so I suggest you don't hang about. I wouldn't want you to be disappointed."

"Thank you very much, Mr Curry," said Paddington doubtfully. "Bears are good at browsing, so I don't expect I shall keep it very long."

But the Browns' neighbour had already disappeared. One moment he was there, the next moment, following what sounded remarkably like a chuckle, his kitchen door slammed shut.

Paddington stood where he was for a moment or two, wondering what to do with the paper in his paw; then he slowly made his way back to the kitchen.

Mrs Bird, the Browns' housekeeper, was busy making marmalade, but she gave one of her snorts when he told her what had happened. "I'll give that Mr Curry a birthday present," she said.

Withdrawing a wooden spoon from one of the saucepans, she licked it with evident relish. "One he won't forget in a hurry."

Catching sight of an anxious look on Paddington's face, she softened. "I daresay he can't help being the way he is. He must have been born that way. It's our bad luck we have the misfortune to live next door to him.

"It isn't like me to forget anyone's birthday," she continued, her mind clearly on other things. "Even Mr Curry's. I thought it was much later in the year…

"Could you read out some of the things he wants – I daren't leave my saucepans for a moment in case they boil over."

Paddington was only too pleased to oblige.

"A new ballcock for the cistern…" he announced, "…a mouse trap… breakfast cereal (see two packets for price of one offer at cut-price grocers)… a three-for-one offer on tubes of shaving cream from new stall in market…"

"I take it all back," said Mrs Bird, over another quick stir. "He must have turned over a new leaf. It doesn't sound like him at all. It's much too modest."

She thought for a moment. "It just so happens I have a fruit cake in the oven. It was meant for our tea, but it won't take long to cover it with marzipan… he likes lots of candles and his name written in the icing…

"It would happen today when I'm up to my eyes. It's way past the marmalade-making season, but I'm experimenting with some Seville oranges I've been keeping in the freezer. I'm not too sure how they will turn out."

"Your 2009s were very good, Mrs Bird," said Paddington knowledgeably. "I stuck three of the labels from the jars into my scrapbook to remind me. It was the best I've ever had."

"All gone, I'm afraid," said Mrs Bird, hiding her

pleasure as best she could over the saucepan. "And there's not much left of the 2010s either. I don't know what happens to marmalade in this house," she added meaningly. "It just disappears."

Clearly in two minds about what to do next, she began sorting out her spoons.

"Perhaps I could help, Mrs Bird?" said Paddington. "I wouldn't want your experiment to go wrong."

"Would you mind, dear?" said Mrs Bird. "You could get him some of that shaving cream." Reaching into her handbag she withdrew a five pound note. "That ought to take care of it."

Paddington needed no second bidding. The steam from the saucepan was making his whiskers droop, and with Mrs Brown at the hairdressers, and both Jonathan and Judy away at school, he was at a bit of a loose end, so he was on his way in no time at all.

Over the years he had become a well-known figure in the Portobello market, and although he had gained a reputation for driving a hard bargain, the resident traders were always pleased to see him.

That said, more often than not, outsiders with

their barrows were a case of 'here today and gone tomorrow', so it was some while before Paddington came across the one he was looking for.

Chalked on a large piece of slate were the words: TODAY'S BARGAIN, and underneath a smaller announcement that said: THREE ORDINARY SIZE TUBES OF SHAVING CREAM ALL IN ONE GIANT TUBE!

"As used by some of the crowned 'eads of Europe in the old days," called the stall keeper, rubbing his hands in anticipation of a sale as he saw Paddington eyeing his display. "It wasn't my fault it fell off the back of a lorry a couple of days ago just as I 'appened to be setting up me barrow. I ran after it, but it was gone before I could say 'alf a mo."

He took a closer look at Paddington. "If you don't mind my saying so," he said. "You look as though you could do with a good shave…

"I'm not asking two nicker. I'm not even asking three. Seeing as you're the first customer of the day, you can 'ave one of them giant tubes for four pounds…"

Paddington gave the man a hard stare. "Aren't you going the wrong way?" he said, raising his hat politely.

The stall keeper paused and his eyes narrowed. "I can see there are no flies on you, mate," he said. "If you don't fancy 'aving a good shave, how about a new titfer tat?" He reached out for a pile of hats. "Yours looks as if it's seen better days."

"It belonged to my uncle in Darkest Peru," said

Paddington. "It was handed down. The shaving cream is a birthday present for our next door neighbour."

Wilting under Paddington's gaze, the man hastily changed his tune. "Nothing like starting the day with a bit of friendly banter," he said. "You can 'ave it for two pounds and seeing it's a birthday present I'll throw in some wrapping paper for luck."

"Thank you very much," said Paddington. "I might come here to do some shopping again tomorrow."

"I might not be 'ere tomorrow," said the man with feeling. "Especially if I get too many customers like you," he added under his breath.

But Paddington was already on his way.

Even if the wrapping paper did look as though it had seen better days, he still thought it was the best morning's shopping he had done for a long while, and he hurried back to number thirty-two Windsor Gardens as fast as his legs would carry him in order to break the news to Mrs Bird and give her the change from her five pound note.

The Browns' housekeeper could hardly believe her eyes when she saw what Paddington had bought. "I've never seen such a big tube," she said. "I do hope you haven't been taken for a ride. Even bears don't get something for nothing these days."

"The man said it was the same as some of the crowned heads of Europe used in the old days," said Paddington.

"That's as may be," said Mrs Bird. "But as I recall, most of them had beards, so there can't have been much demand for it."

"Perhaps that's why they had a lot left over," said Paddington.

"Perhaps," said Mrs Bird. It sounded like typical salesman's patter to her, but she didn't want to be a wet blanket.

However, her words weighed heavily on Paddington's mind as he made his way upstairs to his bedroom.

Removing the tube from its box, he examined it carefully. There was no sign of a dent, but if it really had fallen off the back of a lorry it might well have become bent.

To make doubly sure all was well, he fetched Mr Brown's special shaving mirror on a stand from the bathroom. Although one side of the glass was just like an ordinary mirror – the other side made things seem much larger than they really were and that was the one he wanted.

Placing the stand carefully in the centre of his bedside table, he laid his old leather suitcase flat on the floor in front of it and picked up Mr Curry's present.

Having climbed on top of the case, he carefully unscrewed the cap on the end of the tube and held the nozzle up to the mirror before giving the tube itself a gentle squeeze.

A tiny white blob the size of a small pea appeared momentarily, then went back inside again.

Paddington stared at the nozzle. Disappearing shaving cream wouldn't be a good start to anyone's day if they were in a hurry. In his mind's eye he could already hear cries of, "Bear! Where are you, bear?" issuing from Mr Curry's bathroom window.

Knowing the Browns' neighbour of old, he would be demanding his money back even though he hadn't paid for it.

Bracing himself, Paddington gritted his teeth and had another go. This time he used both paws and gave the tube a much harder squeeze.

For a moment or two nothing happened and he was about to give up when he felt a minor explosion in his paw and a stream of white foamy liquid shot everywhere. It left Mr Brown's mirror looking as though it had been buried by a major blizzard at the North Pole.

Paddington was so taken by surprise he let go of the tube like a hot cake and hovered to and fro on top of his suitcase before finally losing his balance.

Stepping backwards into space, it could only have been a split second or so before he landed on the floor, but the tube had beaten him to it.

As he lay where he had fallen, his legs and arms waving helplessly in the air, he was aware of a further eruption, and through half-closed eyes he saw what remained of the tube's contents flying in all directions.

The largest lump of all hit the ceiling right above his head, and as it slowly detached itself, Paddington jumped to his feet.

He gazed mournfully round the room. It was a long time since he had seen it in quite such a mess, and it had all come about in the twinkling of an eye; so fast, in fact, there was nothing he could possibly have done to stop it.

Hastily returning Mr Brown's mirror to the bathroom before anything else untoward happened, Paddington held it under the tap for a while before returning it to its rightful place.

It took rather longer than he had bargained for, because the hot water made the cream turn into foam and he was soon enveloped in bubbles. That was another thing about messes; they tended to spread, and the more you tried to put things right the worse they became.

It was while he was drying everything as best he could with the towels that his gaze alighted on a wall cabinet above the basin. He knew from past explorations that it was full of interesting things in bottles and packets, but apart from a small spoon and some nail files, he couldn't remember there being any other likely tools. All the same, he took them back to his bedroom, just in case.

Once there, he consulted the instructions on the side of the tube. There was a great deal on the subject of what a wonderful shaving experience lay in wait for the user, but there was nothing at all about how to get the cream back into the tube if too much had come out.

Removing as much as he could from the walls and the furniture before getting down to work, Paddington soon discovered it wasn't as easy as he had expected.

Holding the tube with one paw and applying shaving cream to the nozzle with the spoon, he couldn't help but grip the tube so tightly to stop it bending that in the end most of the cream landed on the floor.

His friend, Mr Gruber, often said that what comes out doesn't necessarily go back in again, and the wisdom of his words was soon confirmed.

In fact, Paddington was concentrating so much on the task in hand he didn't hear Mrs Bird until she was outside his room.

"How are you getting on with wrapping Mr Curry's present?" she called.

"I haven't even started on that, Mrs Bird," said Paddington.

Opening the door as little as possible, he peered through the gap.

"Do you have to do it in your bedroom?" asked Mrs Bird.

"I do now," said Paddington sadly.

"Well, let me know if you need a hand with the knots," said Mrs Bird. "I shan't be long. I've run out of candles for Mr Curry's cake, and I don't doubt he'll be counting them. I'd better make sure I use enough or that'll be wrong. On the other hand, I don't want to use too many and risk him catching the house on fire.

"I haven't even started on the lettering yet. If anyone phones, tell them I shall be back in a quarter of an hour or so."

Mrs Bird sounded flustered, as well she might

with all that was going on, but after a short pause, Paddington heard the sound of the front door closing and as it did, so it triggered off another of his ideas.

Hurrying downstairs, he made his way to the kitchen and there, sure enough, lay the answer to his problem. Mr Curry's freshly-iced cake was sitting in the middle of the table, and alongside it was exactly what he needed: a canvas bag on the end of which there was a tiny metal funnel. It must have been meant.

"I think," said Mr Brown, over tea in the garden the following week, "my handiwork with the fence must have paid off. I haven't seen old Curry looking over it for ages."

"I'm afraid it's a bit more complicated than that, Henry," replied Mrs Brown. "It's all to do with his birthday."

"If I hadn't been in such a rush the morning after Paddington planted his seeds, I wouldn't have stopped him in the middle of what Mr Curry said was a list of the presents he wanted," agreed Mrs Bird.

"When I had the chance to take a proper look it had things on it like a tin of peas…"

"And half a cabbage!" added Paddington indignantly. "It was his shopping list, and we bought him a present too!"

"Hold on a minute," said Mr Brown. "What has all that got to do with the garden fence?"

"He dropped the list over our side of the fence…" explained Mrs Brown.

"Accidentally on purpose," broke in Mrs Bird. "It happened to land at Paddington's feet and Mr Curry said it was his birthday list."

"In that case he deserves all he got!" said Mr Brown, rising to Paddington's defence. "Er… what *did* we give him in the end?"

"A tube marked 'shaving cream', which was full of icing sugar," said Mrs Bird, "and a cake with his name written across the top in shaving cream. I can't think that either of them went down very well, but it serves him right for playing such a mean trick."

"I had an accident with the tube," explained Paddington, "so I borrowed Mrs Bird's cake-making outfit to get the shaving cream back inside it. Only the bag still had some icing sugar inside it so I put that into the tube by mistake."

"And when I came to use it," said Mrs Bird, "I didn't realise Paddington had filled it with shaving cream. I couldn't think why it wouldn't set."

"Which, as things turned out," said Mrs Brown, "meant that for once Mr Curry couldn't have his cake and eat it too. Perhaps it's taught him a lesson. We haven't had sight nor sound of him since. Let's hope it lasts."

"Pigs might fly," snorted Mrs Bird.

"So that's how I came to have traces of shaving cream over my bathroom mirror," said Mr Brown. "I thought something must have been going on…

"Hold on a moment," he continued, as light suddenly dawned. "Did you say all this happened last Wednesday?"

"I did," said Mrs Brown. "Why do you ask, Henry?"

"Because," said Mr Brown, "last Wednesday was April the first. You can play any tricks you like before midday. If you ask me, not only was Mr Curry playing an April fool trick, but whoever sold Paddington the shaving cream was probably doing much the same thing."

"They didn't bargain on the fact that there are some bears who happen to have been born under a lucky star," said Mrs Brown. "Now we are enjoying some peace and quiet for a change, so all's well that ends well."

And that was something no one could argue with, especially when they saw that seemingly almost overnight Paddington's seeds had begun to sprout. It was nice having things to look forward to.

Chapter Two

A Fishy Business

Paddington's best friend, Mr Gruber, was most sympathetic when he heard about the goings on at number thirty-two Windsor Gardens.

"It's no wonder I didn't see as much of you as usual last week, Mr Brown," he said. "I must say my elevenses didn't feel the same without our having cocoa and buns together.

"Playing a simple jape on someone because it's April Fools' Day is one thing, but trying to get something for nothing is another matter entirely.

"That Mr Curry deserves all he gets," he added, echoing Mrs Bird's words.

"As for the man who sold you the shaving cream, words fail me."

"He wasn't there this morning," said Paddington. "I was hoping I might get Mrs Bird's money back for her."

"Good riddance to bad rubbish," said Mr Gruber, busying himself at the stove in the back of his shop. "That kind of person gives the market a bad name. The only good thing is they never stay in one place for very long. It's like I always say, 'here today and gone tomorrow'."

He handed Paddington a steaming mug of cocoa.

"You must have been quite worn out by it all, Mr Brown. I dare say you didn't get much sleep last night."

"I was still awake at nine o'clock," said Paddington.

"Well, there you are," said Mr Gruber. He settled himself down alongside his friend on the old horsehair sofa at the back of the shop. "That kind of thing isn't good for a young bear."

Paddington sipped his cocoa thoughtfully. There was something very comforting about Mr Gruber's antique shop. Although it was full of old things, there was always something new to look at. In fact, it was an ever changing scene. As fast as one item disappeared, something else came along to take its place, so it was never entirely the same two days running.

Today was a good example. An old wind-up gramophone that had enjoyed pride of place on a table in the centre of the shop for several weeks had disappeared. In its place there was a very strange-looking picture which appeared to have been made by someone glueing a mish-mash of different bits and pieces on to a board and then pouring paint all over it.

Paddington was much too polite to say so, but he preferred the old wind-up gramophone with a dog peering into a huge horn to see where the sound was coming from when it was working. The dog had looked so real he'd often been tempted to offer it one of his buns.

"That picture is what is known as a *collage*," said Mr Gruber, reading Paddington's thoughts. "It's made of various bits and pieces glued together in a random fashion. The idea itself is as old as the hills. In fact, many famous artists started out that way... Picasso... Salvador Dali...

"It may look very modern, but I think it is probably older than it seems. In which case it could be very valuable. It's called Sunset in Tahiti."

Paddington thought it looked more like a rainy day in the Bayswater Road, but he didn't say anything.

Mr Gruber knew much more about these things than he did, and he listened carefully as his friend explained the ins and outs of the subject while they had their elevenses.

"What makes it particularly interesting," continued Mr Gruber, "is that someone else has painted over the original picture – which often happened at one time, but they were using a method known as egg *tempera*, which is why it looks so shiny."

Paddington licked his lips. "I've never heard of a painting made with eggs," he said.

"There are other things besides," said Mr Gruber. "Vinegar, various pigments to provide the colour – and in this case some graphite too, which you can find in any bicycle puncture repair outfit…"

"I wouldn't mind having a go at making one of those myself," said Paddington. "But I expect it's a bit difficult with paws and I can't think what I would make a picture of anyway."

Mr Gruber eyed Paddington over his mug of cocoa. It was unlike his friend to admit defeat before he had even begun something.

"You do yourself an injustice, Mr Brown," he said. "There is no such word as *can't*."

"When we are out for a drive Mr Brown sometimes says the road has a nasty *cant*," said Paddington. "I thought he meant he had just driven over a tin can."

"That's the English language for you," said Mr Gruber. "The word 'cant' pronounced one way means a road has a slant to it, but that same word with an apostrophe between the last two letters is short for 'cannot', meaning it is not possible.

"I think all things are possible if you really set your mind to it, and you never know what you can do until you try.

"As for finding a subject for your painting..." Mr Gruber rose to his feet as he saw someone about to enter his shop, "...you only have to take a short ride on the top deck of a London bus and all manner of things cry out to be painted: the world is your oyster."

Having said goodbye to his friend for the time being, Paddington was about to head back home, when he had second thoughts.

The sun was shining and for once, instead of his shopping basket on wheels, he only had his suitcase, so as soon as he came across a bus stop, he held out a paw and stopped the first one that came into view.

As the doors opened he climbed aboard and headed for the stairs.

"And where do you think you're going, young-feller-me-bear?" called the driver.

"Nowhere in particular, thank you very much," said Paddington. "I'm looking for ideas."

"Well you've picked the right route for not going anywhere in particular, I'll say that," said the driver gloomily. "We've been stuck in traffic jams all the morning." He pointed to a long line of waiting cars ahead of them. "It's all them roadworks. Never-ending they are, and as fast as they fill one hole in, someone else comes along and digs it up again."

"I'm looking for something to paint," said Paddington, raising his hat politely.

"That's as may be," said the driver, not unkindly. "And I promise not to tell anyone if they ask. But you're not doing any of it on my bus – not without a ticket. Rembrandt 'imself wouldn't be allowed on without one. It's as much as my job's worth if an inspector gets on.

"If I might make a suggestion," he continued, "you'd be better off painting a picture of one of them holes near where you were standing. It's what they call a still life."

Paddington was about to explain that he needed some eggs first, but he thought better of it. He wasn't too sure how to go about it himself without a book of instructions.

"I thought you might give me a ticket," he said. "I can pay for it."

Having made sure nobody was looking over his shoulder, he opened his suitcase and felt inside the secret compartment.

"It's a sixpence," he explained, holding up a small coin gleaming in the morning sun for the driver to see. "I've been keeping it polished for a rainy day."

"When was the last time you travelled on a bus, mate?" asked the driver. "Even if it was raining cats and dogs, which it isn't, and even if your coin was valid, which it isn't – it wouldn't take you any further than the next stop… if that. Besides, you have to get a ticket from a machine. I don't carry them."

He took a closer look at the coin. "It isn't even a sixpence!" he exclaimed. "It's a Peruvian centavo."

"I've never been on a bus by myself before," admitted Paddington. "They don't have any in Darkest Peru, and whenever I've travelled on one in London it's usually been with Mr Gruber on one of his outings, and he insists on paying."

Hearing an outbreak of tooting from behind as the traffic in front showed signs of moving, the bus driver reached for his dashboard.

"Well," he said, since I'm not in a position of being able to wait around on the off chance your Mr Gruber might come past, I suggest you take yourself on an outing right now and vacate the platform. I've got a busy schedule to keep up and we're running late as it is.

"If you're going to be doing a lot of travelling," he added, "your best bet is to get yourself an Oyster."

Paddington pricked up his ears. "Mr Gruber says you can go anywhere in the world on an oyster," he exclaimed excitedly.

"I wouldn't go as far as to say that, not in this traffic," said the driver. "But in principle you can go wherever you like within the Greater London area."

With that he pressed a button and a metallic voice from somewhere inside the bus called out, 'Stand Clear. Doors Closing. Stand Clear. Doors Closing'.

Paddington scrambled out of harm's way, and then stared after the bus as it pulled away from the kerb and continued on its journey for a few more yards.

He sat down on his suitcase at the side of the road for a moment or two in order to consider his next move.

Mr Brown was right. Only the other day he had been saying that what with credit cards and computers and something called 'shopping on the net' it wouldn't be very long before paying for things with real money would be a thing of the past, but he hadn't mentioned the possibility of having to use an oyster to get on a bus. It was no wonder he went on an underground train when he travelled to and fro from his office in the city.

With that thought uppermost in his mind, Paddington picked up his suitcase and set off for the nearest fishmongers.

Overtaking the bus which was held up by yet another hole in the road, he raised his hat to the driver, who gave him a gloomy thumbs up sign in return, and shortly afterwards, having reached a row of shops, he made for the one he had in mind. It was where Mrs Bird went whenever she was shopping for fish.

"I would like an oyster, please," he announced,

raising his hat politely to a boy behind the counter, who was busy making sure all the fish heads were facing the same way.

"There's a young foreign gent wants an oyster," repeated the boy over his shoulder.

"I'd like a day return one, if I may," added Paddington, trying to be helpful.

"I'm afraid we don't get any returns here," said the assistant. "They're fresh in from France twice a week and once they're gone they're gone..."

"In that case I'd better have two," said Paddington. "One for going and one for coming back."

The assistant didn't actually say 'we've got the last of the big spenders here', but his look said it all. "I'll have to ask the manager," he said.

"He wants two!" he called. "One for going and one for coming back. I think it's some kind of outing.

"We usually sell them by the dozen," he explained, addressing Paddington, "and the only returns you get is if there's a bad one, and if that happens you'll wish you'd never gone wherever it was in the first place. Ho! Ho! Ho!"

"Tell him there aren't many around at the moment," shouted a voice from the back of the shop. "And there won't be any at all soon when there isn't an R in the month."

The assistant repeated the message for Paddington's benefit.

Paddington gave him a hard stare. "There isn't an M in a lot of months," he said. "But that doesn't stop Mrs Bird giving me marmalade for breakfast."

"Tell him we've got some kippers," shouted the

manager. "Fresh in this morning."

"Can you get very far on a kipper?" asked Paddington hopefully.

"You can if you set light to its tail and hang on tight," said the assistant. "Ho! Ho! Ho!"

"We don't normally have oysters all through the summer," said the manager, as he emerged from a back room to see what was going on. "It's the breeding season."

"It must make travelling difficult in August," said Paddington.

"Er... yes," said the manager, not wishing to commit himself.

"As a matter of interest," he continued. "Where are you from exactly? I only ask because we don't get much call for oysters at this time of the year. They aren't at their best and if it's for some kind of national celebration..."

"I'm from Peru," said Paddington. "Darkest Peru."

"Darkest Peru!" repeated the manager. "Well, I suppose you wouldn't get many oysters in the jungle."

"I saw a film about Peruvian bears on television the other night," broke in the assistant. "They were going through people's dustbins after dark. But I don't think they were after oysters."

Paddington gave the assistant another hard stare. "I've never, ever, gone through anyone's dustbin after dark!" he exclaimed hotly. "Mrs Bird would be most upset."

"Mrs Bird?" repeated the manager. "Of number thirty-two Windsor Gardens? Why ever didn't you say so in the first place? She's one of our best customers.

"Seeing he knows Mrs Bird, you'd better stretch a point and give him a couple," he continued, addressing his assistant. "Anything for a quiet life," he added in a whisper.

"Two pounds five each . . . that'll be four pounds ten pee." said the assistant.

"Four pounds ten pee," repeated Paddington, nearly falling over backwards with alarm.

"Don't worry," said the manager hastily. "I'll put it down on her account."

"Would you like them gift wrapped?" asked the assistant.

"Shh," said the manager, glaring at him.

"Thank you very much," said Paddington, "but I shall need one straight away."

Only seconds before he had seen a red bus go past, and sure enough, it had stopped a little way along the road. A small queue of people were already boarding it through a door near the driver.

"Wait for me!" he called.

Luck was with him, for just as he heard a by-now familiar voice calling out, 'Stand Clear. Doors Closing', he caught sight of another opening in the side of the bus and before the message was repeated, he scrambled through it in the nick of time.

"Dear me," said a lady on a seat just inside. "Are you all right?"

Paddington raised his hat. "I think so," he said. "But I was in a hurry because I want to test my oysters."

"I think you will find there are some seats upstairs," began the lady haughtily, but before she had a chance to say any more a rather less than friendly voice made an announcement.

"Will the person who has just boarded the bus through the door marked Exit kindly report to the driver!"

Paddington made his way to the front of the bus. "I was wanting to test one of my oysters," he explained. "I've never used one before and I need to do it while there is still an R in the month."

"Well, hurry up," said the driver. "At this rate it won't be long before it's May." He pointed to a large yellow button on the side of his cabin. "Show it to the electronic reader."

"I didn't know oysters could read," said Paddington.

"You learn something new every day," said the driver. "Now, hurry up so we can get on our way."

"Hear! Hear!" came a voice from the back of the bus. "Some of us have got trains to catch."

"I won't report you on this occasion," continued the driver, "but don't do it again. I haven't got all day."

Carefully undoing the wrapping on his package, Paddington removed one of the oysters and pressed the inside of it against the button as hard as he could, twisting it first of all in a clockwise direction, so that it made good contact. Then, because despite the hard shell it felt rather softer than he had expected, he tried turning it the other way.

As he stood back and removed the shell a stream of liquid oozed on to the floor.

"I'm afraid your bus doesn't seem to be moving," he said. "I think there must be something wrong with it."

"I said show it to the reader, not grind it into the works," said the driver.

His nose twitched as he leaned over the side of his cabin to take a closer look.

He stared at the object in Paddington's paw as though he couldn't believe his eyes.

"That's a blooming oyster!" he bellowed. "Ugh! Look at it! No wonder it didn't work! Wait till the inspector sees what you've done! He'll have your guts for garters!

"That settles it. We can't go any further. Everybody off! Everybody off!" He pressed a button, and the disembodied voice began uttering the words, 'Stand Clear. Doors Opening. Stand Clear. Doors Opening'.

A moment later all was chaos.

Being in pole position, Paddington was the first to leave, and he didn't stop running until he reached the safety of the Portobello Road.

Mr Gruber looked most concerned as Paddington burst into his shop, and having made sure there was no one else behind him, stood there mopping his brow with a handkerchief.

"Whatever is the matter, Mr Brown?" he asked. "You look as though you've been in an earthquake."

"I've been having trouble with my oysters," said Paddington.

"What are garters, Mr Gruber?" he gasped as soon as he could get his breath back.

"They are things gentlemen use to keep their socks up," said Mr Gruber. "Why do you ask, Mr Brown?"

"Well," said Paddington. "The driver of the last bus I was on said his inspector would have my guts to make a pair of them if he ever caught up with me."

"Oh dear," said Mr Gruber. "You had better tell me all."

And while he set about making the second helping of cocoa that morning, Paddington related all that had happened to him since they had last seen each other.

"I would say it isn't so much the oysters that have been the cause of all the trouble," said Mr Gruber, when Paddington had finished. "It's the English language again. We live in an age when people will insist on shortening things. In your case, I'm sure with the best of intentions, your driver suggested you should buy an oyster rather than an Oyster *card*. I will show you one."

Reaching into his wallet he produced an old card to show what he meant.

Paddington looked very downcast by the time Mr Gruber had finished. "It's no wonder people didn't know what I was talking about," he said. "Now I've got my return oyster left over and I don't suppose anyone will ever want to eat it."

Mr Gruber stirred his cocoa thoughtfully. "All is not lost, Mr Brown," he said. "I have a suggestion to make…"

"I think," said Mrs Bird, a few days later, "before you are very much older, Paddington, you had better bring whatever you have made downstairs to show the rest of us."

It being the weekend, all the family were present and at her suggestion they gathered together on the lawn.

"Good heavens!" exclaimed Mr Brown, as Paddington held up his handiwork. Don't tell me you made that all by yourself. Er…what is it?"

"Whatever it is, it's better out than in if you ask me," said Mrs Brown.

"It's what's known as a *collage*," said Paddington, knowledgeably. "A *collage* with an overlay of some eggs and graphite *tempera*."

"Good gracious," said Mrs Bird. "Whatever next? As for using eggs... I thought I was running low."

"No wonder you wanted to borrow my bicycle puncture outfit," Jonathan chimed in. "There I was, thinking your hot-water bottle must have sprung a leak."

"It looks wonderful," said Judy loyally. "Whatever gave you the idea?"

"It's a long story," said Paddington vaguely. "It's to do with not going anywhere on a bus."

"But what is it meant to be?" persisted Mr Brown.

"Mr Curry on a bad day?" suggested Jonathan.

"The oyster in the middle looks so real," said Mrs Brown. "And the inside of the shell is so shiny it looks good enough to eat."

"I wouldn't if I were you, Mrs Brown," said Paddington.

Mrs Bird sniffed the air. "If I might make a suggestion," she said. "It's like a lot of modern paintings. They are at their best if you stand well away from them. Why don't we hang it down the end of the garden for the time being?"

But it was Mr Gruber who paid Paddington the best compliment of all. He stood it on the table in his shop alongside the picture that had started it all.

"It bears out what I have always said about there being no such word as *can't*," he said. "I doubt if

Picasso at his peak could have produced anything better."

"So it could be worth a lot of money," said Paddington excitedly.

"Not just yet, I'm afraid," said Mr Gruber. "Very often it's a matter of waiting until the creator is no longer with us."

"I could do the rest of my shopping, if you like?" said Paddington.

"I think it might take even longer than that, Mr Brown," said his friend tactfully.

For a while lots of passers-by dropped in to admire Paddington's handiwork, but as the weather grew warmer it was noticeable that fewer and fewer actually entered the shop and if they did, they didn't linger.

There came a time when even Mr Gruber began to have second thoughts.

"If you have no objection, Mr Brown," he said. "I may find another home for your masterpiece." And he hung Paddington's work on a tree in the tiny patio behind his shop.

First of all he made a photocopy of it for his

shop window, and alongside it was a notice saying: VIEWING BY APPOINTMENT ONLY.

Acting on Mr Gruber's advice, Paddington added his special paw print in the bottom right hand corner, just to show it was a genuine original.

Chapter Three

SPRING-CLEANING

ALTHOUGH MRS BIRD ran what Mr Brown often called 'a tight ship' (usually brought on by her sighs when he came in from the garden and deposited mud all over her newly polished kitchen floor), it would have been nearer the truth to say that she did her best to keep everything shipshape and tidy at number thirty-two Windsor Gardens, which wasn't always easy.

Not that she was in the habit of laying down the law on such matters. In her view a happy household was one where everyone felt free to do as they wished; within reason of course. Also, it was a matter of territories.

That said, very little untoward escaped her eagle eye and she was a past-mistress in the art of raising her eyebrows to good effect. The Browns could tell at once by the look on her face when things were not to her liking.

So when she happened to glance into Paddington's bedroom one morning and her eyebrows soared heavenwards to their fullest extent, he wasn't at all surprised. In fact, for a moment or two he thought they might disappear altogether over the back of her head.

His own eyebrows had recently been doing much the same thing when he woke in the morning and he saw the state of his room. It always looked much worse by daylight, but by the time he reached his dressing table mirror his brows were usually in their normal place and try as he might he couldn't see any joins.

The simple fact was that ever since the debacle over Mr Curry's birthday present, followed by his efforts at creating the oyster montage, he had been putting off tidying up.

His Aunt Lucy, who in many ways was not unlike Mrs Bird, would have recognised the signs immediately. It was what she would have called a bad attack of the *mañanas* – the Spanish word for tomorrow, and as everyone knows, there are times when 'tomorrow never comes'.

Paddington braced himself for the worst, but for once Mrs Bird seemed at a loss for words. Pursing her lips, she closed the door and disappeared downstairs, only to return a few minutes later armed with a dustpan and brush and a bucketful of cleaning materials.

"It's the first day of the summer sales," she said, "and Jonathan and Judy are coming home for the school holidays tomorrow, so Mrs Brown and I are going out to look for some new curtain material while we have the chance.

"That being so, I'm afraid lunch will be later than usual, which may be no bad thing. It will give you more time to make your room spick-and-span by the time we get back. And when we do, I don't want to see any marmalade stains or dried oyster juice, and none of that dreadful shaving cream which seems to have gone everywhere except where it's supposed to.

"I don't know what Mr Brown will say if he ever gets to see the state your room is in.

"And don't forget to clean under the bed!"

With that parting shot she closed the door.

"Do you think it wise leaving Paddington to his own devices for such a long time?" asked Mrs Brown, as they left the house. "Remember the old saying – 'the devil finds work for idle paws'?"

"You haven't seen the state of his room," said Mrs Bird, "it's worse than that of an average teenage boy, and that's saying something. Remember what Jonathan's room used to look like before he went off to boarding school?"

Mrs Brown gave a sigh. "You couldn't see the floor for junk. He used to stand all his jeans in a row by the side of the bed and step into the pair he fancied most next morning."

"Don't remind me," said Mrs Bird. "At least Paddington hangs his duffle coat on its proper hook at night. As for being left to his own devices, that bear's paws won't be idle for the rest of the day. It's a long time since his room had a thorough going-over, and he can't come to much harm with a dustpan and brush and a few old scrubbing brushes. Besides, the exercise will do him good."

"How about the vacuum cleaner?" asked Mrs Brown, recalling the time when Paddington had put the tube in the wrong end and blown soot all over the dining room carpet.

"Locked away in a cupboard," said Mrs Bird. "And the key's in my handbag.

"As for the carpet... if you remember, when it was first laid it was done in a rush by Mr Briggs, and he didn't even bother with any proper underlay. He left the old newspapers in place and added a few more for good measure. One way and another the room needs a good going-over by a proper decorator."

"Oh dear," said Mrs Brown. "I keep asking Henry to do something about it, but he can be very forgetful when it suits him."

"That's as may be," said Mrs Bird, "but as for taking Paddington with us, he would be bored stiff in no time at all. Besides, he's probably hard at work already."

Mrs Bird spoke with the voice of experience, although for once she failed to take account of a bear's priorities.

The sound of the front door being closed had hardly died away before Paddington hurried downstairs in order to make a plentiful supply of marmalade sandwiches ahead of the day's work.

Once he was back in his room, he looked for a safe place to put them in case any dust clouds landed on top while his back was turned.

Only then did he fill the bucket with hot water from the bathroom, and having put his pyjamas back on in case he got his fur wet, he rolled up the sleeves and began work on his bedroom walls with a scrubbing brush and a bar of soap.

Paddington was an optimistic bear in many ways, but he had to admit it was a bit of a setback when no sooner had he applied a scrubbing brush to

the paper than it began to come away from the wall. Worse still, the more he scrubbed the worse it became. In what seemed like no time at all, he was literally knee-deep in paper, and even allowing for the fact that bears' knees were fairly near the floor, it was still a sizeable amount.

Having decided that perhaps it had been a mistake to use the hot tap rather than the cold, Paddington sat down on the edge of his bed and gazed around the room.

In many respects it was the reverse of what had happened soon after he went to live with the Browns and offered to help Mr Brown with the decorating.

On that occasion, apart from adding too much water to the paste, he managed to paper over the door by mistake and had been unable to find his way out. Now the same door was practically the only part left untouched.

Unfortunately he spent so much time wondering if perhaps his adding too much water to the paste all that time ago was the cause of his present problem, he failed to notice some large chunks of paper had somehow or other contrived to stick themselves back on the wall again. Some had done so at a very peculiar angle indeed, and when he tried to straighten out the worst of them, bits came away in his paw and stuck to his pyjamas instead.

Catching sight of his reflection in the dressing table mirror, Paddington decided to give cleaning walls a miss for the time being and concentrate instead on doing the dusting.

Pushing the bed to one side, he found Mrs Bird was right about one thing. The area of carpet where it had been looked particularly fruitful, and the pan was soon half-full of dust, not to mention several old Liquorice Allsorts into the bargain. They had gone missing some months previously, along with various other small items he had forgotten all about.

By then the dust was making his nose itch, and one of the Allsorts was on the point of going down the wrong way. Fearing if he didn't do something quickly he might drop the pan, he glanced around the room and noticed that in moving the bed away from the skirting board the carpet had risen up at one point.

At first sight it seemed an ideal place to store the contents of the pan for the time being, especially as there appeared to be some newspapers lining the floorboards, so in desperation he opened up the gap still further and managed to upend the pan a split second before the inevitable happened.

A loud *tishoooo* echoed round the bedroom, and as it did so a small cloud of dust rose from the very spot where it had just landed.

He waited a moment or two for it to settle before bending down to brush it back into the pan and while he was doing so he glanced idly at the papers.

Paddington wasn't normally a great reader of newspapers. On the whole he much preferred magazines. Newspapers were rather difficult with paws. Even if you did come across something interesting to read, more often than not the pages were stuck together, and no amount of blowing would make them come apart.

However, for once he had to admit the papers on the floor looked unusually inviting. Some of them were fairly up-to-date, whereas others must have been there for a very long time because in the pictures everyone was wearing a hat, and motor cars looked different; like a lot of boxes on wheels. Some were even drawn by horses, and in one picture there was a man on a bicycle that had one enormous wheel at the front and a tiny one at the back.

Those things apart, there wasn't a coloured picture to be seen; everything, including the advertisements, was black and white.

Pulling back the carpet still further, Paddington couldn't help thinking Mr Gruber might like some of the older newspapers for his antique shop, and he was wondering whether or not he should mention it to the Browns, when his eye was caught by an item on cookery in one of the more up-to-date editions.

But it wasn't just any old cooking... it was all about food in foreign countries, and... Paddington grew more and more excited as he read on... It was about things people ate in South America... including... he nearly fell over backwards with excitement... there was a picture of a special cake they had sometimes been given for a treat in the Home for Retired Bears. It even had the recipe printed below it.

Having taken a quick look over his shoulder to make sure no one was watching, he carefully removed the item from the newspaper, and as he did so he had another idea.

Paddington was very keen on cooking. Of late Mrs Bird often let him help out with things like stirring the batter when she was making a Yorkshire pudding to go with the Sunday lunch, and by general agreement he was a dab hand at making gravy. But she usually drew the line when it came to doing anything more complicated by himself, largely on account of the fact that he was always wanting to test the results long before they were ready, and she didn't want him to singe his whiskers by opening the oven door too soon.

It struck Paddington that he might never again have such a golden opportunity to do-it-all-by-himself. After a hard day at the sales, what could be nicer for Mrs Brown and Mrs Bird than to arrive home loaded with shopping only to open the front door and be met by the smell of freshly-baked cakes?

It would also make a nice change from tidying his room.

He read through the list of ingredients: two cupfuls of self-raising flour, the same amount of cornflour, icing sugar, butter, the yolk of an egg, sugar, condensed milk... He wasn't too sure about the condensed milk, otherwise he felt sure Mrs Bird would have all the other items in her larder.

Paddington didn't believe in doing things by half, and it took him some while to assemble all the ingredients. In fact he soon lost count of the number of times he went up and down the stairs carrying them all, and he began to wish he had set to work on making it in the kitchen rather than his bedroom. Wide though his windowsill was, it now resembled the display counter in a grocery shop. On the other hand, he didn't want to be caught in the act if Mrs Brown and Mrs Bird arrived back early.

Having emptied a whole bag of flour into a large mound on the sill, he did the same with the cornflour before turning his attention to the rest of the instructions.

For a second or two he stared at the piece of paper in his paw as though he could hardly believe his eyes. In fact, he turned it over several times in order to make sure he had the right side.

But no, in black and white at the end of the list of contents were the words '. . . continued on page 22'.

Paddington stared at it in disgust. The page he had removed the recipe from was number 7 and there were so many other newspapers mixed up together the chance of finding number 22 would have taken a month of Sundays. Instead of saying 'continued on page 22' it might just as well have said 'continued next week' or 'next month', or worse still… 'never again in a million years'.

Worn-out, and hot and flustered by all his exertions, Paddington reached up to open the window for a draught of fresh air, and immediately wished he hadn't.

Over the years he had often wondered why some flour was called 'self-raising'. Now, in the space of a few seconds, the answer lay before him. It didn't seem possible that such a small quantity of white powder could cover such a large area in such a small amount of time all by itself, but everything in the room now had a thin coating of white.

Hastily closing the window before anything worse happened, Paddington drew the curtains in the vain hope that it might improve matters, and took to his bed.

Tired out, hungry and at the end of his tether, he flopped down on it and lay where he had landed for a moment or two, gazing at the ceiling.

To say that his room was in a worse state than it had ever been before was putting it mildly. It was like a nightmare. In fact it was much worse; at least with a nightmare you woke up at the end and found there was nothing to worry about.

In the past Paddington had often noticed that relaxing wasn't always as easy as it sounded. Flies, for example, often waited until you had settled yourself in the most comfortable position, before landing on the end of your nose. Or, worse still, some part of you developed an itch which wouldn't go away.

Today was no exception, except it wasn't a fly or even an itch, it was more of a lump, and it was in the middle of his back. He couldn't remember there ever being a lump in his bed before and he began feeling underneath his pyjamas to find out what it could possibly be.

Whatever it was, it certainly wasn't hard… if

anything it was soft and… not so much soft, as wet and sticky. It was oozing stickiness, the kind of stickiness that was all too familiar and could mean only one thing.

He remembered now where he had put his marmalade sandwiches for safekeeping!

"I didn't realise you'd washed the sheets before we came out," said Mrs Brown, when they arrived back from their shopping.

Mrs Bird joined her at the kitchen window. "I didn't!" she said grimly, as she surveyed a range of assorted linen hanging on the revolving clothesline.

Her eyes softened as she couldn't help but notice

on a line separate from the rest, a small pair of flowered pyjamas.

She glanced around her kitchen. "Nor, for that matter, did I leave half the cupboard doors open, or a sink full of egg shells."

"Oh dear," said Mrs Brown.

"Oh dear, is right," said Mrs Bird, making her way upstairs.

"You can come out now, wherever you are," she called, as she entered Paddington's room.

The wardrobe door slowly opened and a head appeared. "How did you know I was in here, Mrs Bird?" asked Paddington.

"Little birds know these things," said the Browns' housekeeper, "and one of them told me." She gazed round the room. "I said you wouldn't be idle while we were out shopping, but I didn't expect to find quite such a mess when we got back."

She hesitated for a moment, lost in thought. "I'm sure you did your best," she said at last. "And you meant well. Those are two of the most important things in life."

"I think I did my worst, Mrs Bird," said

Paddington sadly.

"Well at least you tried," said Mrs Bird. "I've no time for people who say they can't do things when they haven't even tried."

While she was talking she caught sight of Paddington's recipe lying on the bed.

"*Alfajores!*" she exclaimed.

"Bless you!" said Paddington.

"That wasn't a sneeze," said Mrs Bird. "It's a dish. I don't believe it. I've been looking everywhere for that recipe ever since you arrived. I wanted to make some for you so that you would feel at home, but I couldn't remember all the ingredients."

"I didn't know that's what they are called," exclaimed Paddington. "But they are very popular in Peru. Everybody has their own recipe. You make a top and a bottom. Then you stick them together with *manjar blanco*."

"What's that when it's at home?" asked Mrs Bird.

"I don't know," admitted Paddington, "Aunt Lucy used to use condensed milk boiled up until it was really thick. They went down well in the

Home for Retired Bears."

"I was thinking of using marmalade," said Mrs Bird. "Thinly spread."

Paddington licked his lips.

"Jonathan and Judy are coming home tomorrow," she continued. "I shall need help from an expert if we're to have enough ready in time. That is, if you wouldn't mind lending a paw."

"Yes, please, Mrs Bird," said Paddington.

"But before that," said Mrs Bird, "we shall need some more eggs."

"It's a bit difficult separating the yolks," said Paddington.

"Well, there you are," said Mrs Bird gravely. "It's useful to know that for a start."

"It strikes me Paddington got off very lightly," said Jonathan when he arrived home and heard the news. "Have you seen his room?"

"It's like Mrs Bird always says," replied Judy. "Bears usually fall on their feet. Have another *alfajore*."

"I don't mind if I do," said Jonathan. "They're very moreish."

"I'll tell you something else," said Judy. "Dad's been on the phone to a decorator. He's coming next week to do Paddington's room."

"You know what that means," said Jonathan.

"He'll be sharing your room for the time being," said Judy.

"I wonder if bears snore?" mused Jonathan. "We could ring the zoo and find out."

"I asked him," said Judy. "He swears they don't. He said he stayed awake one night to find out and he didn't snore once."

"Thanks a heap," said Jonathan.

"Who would have thought Mrs Bird would take it all quite so well?" said Mr Brown later that night.

"Do you know what, Henry?" said Mrs Brown. "I think it was the sight of Paddington's pyjamas hanging all by themselves on the line when we got home. Little things mean a lot to Mrs Bird."

Chapter Four

A CHANCE ENCOUNTER

PADDINGTON PUT ON a spurt as he entered the
Portobello Road, rounding the corner faster than he
had ever done before. In fact, not to put too fine a
point on it, anyone watching would have said he had
momentarily lost control of his shopping basket on
wheels.

The last part of the journey had been downhill

and his legs were going so fast he had difficulty in stopping. Having put the basket into a one-wheel drift, he only just missed colliding with a man standing in the middle of the pavement.

It was most unusual for anyone to be there at that time of the day; the crowds of sightseers didn't normally begin to arrive until much later when all the shops and stalls were open for business.

As it was, his basket ended up on its side. Luckily it was empty, but one of its wheels was still spinning.

"You want to watch where you're going," said the man crossly. "This isn't a racetrack, you know."

"It's a bit difficult with paws," admitted Paddington. "Especially going round corners."

The man stared at him. "I don't see what paws have to do with it," he growled.

Paddington felt tempted to say that was because the man didn't have any, but he was much too polite.

Instead, he stood back and eyed the stranger with interest. Despite the warm weather, he was wearing what looked like plastic muffs over his ears, and having blown into the end of a furry object on the end of a stick, he began counting out loud. "One, two, three, four…" he said, until finally, having reached number ten, he stopped as though at a loss for words.

"I think you will find it's eleven," said Paddington, anxious to make amends for nearly running him over.

The man gave him a glassy stare and put a finger to his lips. He seemed about to reply when the rear doors of a dark green van parked nearby opened and a second man poked his head out.

"OK for sound," he called, giving the thumbs up sign.

He nodded towards Paddington before closing the door. "The early bird catches the worm and you've got to start somewhere. May as well give it a whirl."

The first man didn't look wildly enthusiastic at the idea, but he put a brave face on it as he dusted himself down.

"Would you mind saying a few words into this?" he asked, holding the furry object under Paddington's nose.

"It tickles my whiskers," replied Paddington.

The van door opened again. This time the second

man spread his arms out wide and raised his head heavenwards.

"I think Adrian would like something a little bit longer," explained the first man.

"Excuse me while I mop my brow," said Paddington.

"Even longer than that, perhaps?" said the man. "He's the director and we need to check our levels for sound."

"The Portobello Road is a bit steep just here," agreed Paddington. "That's why I was going so fast."

"Er… yes…" said the man. "But…"

"Mr Gruber is always saying if we have a really bad storm there's going to be a nasty accident one of these days. The water sometimes runs past his shop doorway like a tidal wave. We nearly lost one of his deck chairs that way. It's lucky we weren't having our elevenses on the pavement at the time. Our buns might have been swept away."

The van door opened yet again and the second man pointed downwards with his thumb, mouthing something at the same time.

"Oh dear," said the first man. "I'm afraid you were

a bit too quick for us that time. I doubt if Adrian had time to get back to his desk. My name's Sunny Climes, by the way, and I'm gathering material for the forthcoming Games."

"Perhaps," he suggested, "you would like to tell us what you had for breakfast. We find with most people that's usually about the right length."

He held out his free hand in order to give Paddington's paw a quick shake, then hastily withdrew it.

"I usually have toast and marmalade..." began Paddington.

"So I gather," said Mr Climes. He removed an initialled handkerchief from his top pocket and unfolded it as best he could with his teeth. "We don't want to get any chunks on our microphone if we can help it, do we? Did you have anything else? A cup of tea to help it on its way perhaps?"

"I'm glad you asked me that, Mr Climes," said Paddington. "I usually have cocoa, but Mrs Bird is spring-cleaning the kitchen this week. Most years she gives it a good going-over in April, but she left it until much later this year.

"She wanted to clean out the refrigerator while she was at it and she was worried the things inside might go off while the door was open, so she put everything out on the kitchen table and said it would be a big help if we used up as much as we could.

"There were several kinds of bacon, three different sorts of sausages, eggs, potato cakes, tomatoes, kippers... a half empty tin of llama pâté. Aunt Lucy sent it to us from Peru last Christmas, but it had gone mouldy..."

"So what was your answer to all that?" broke in Mr Climes, trying to get a word in edgeways.

"Thank you very much," said Paddington.

"Don't tell me you ate a bit of everything," exclaimed the interviewer. "The breakfast table must have been full to overflowing with plates."

"No," said Paddington. "Mrs Bird managed to get all mine on two large ones. Besides, I didn't have any kippers in case I got a bone in my throat. I thought I did once and Mrs Brown had to call a doctor, but it turned out to be an old marmalade chunk that had gone hard. It must have fallen out of my hat."

"I'm sorry…" broke in Sunny Climes. Edging away from Paddington, he stationed himself on the other side of a nearby lamppost. "Would you mind holding it there…"

"I'm afraid I can't quite reach it," said Paddington hurrying round the other side of the lamppost to avoid climbing over his shopping basket on wheels.

"I don't mean the microphone," said Mr Climes, moving back the way he had come. Putting a finger to his lips he listened to a command over the headphones. "We seem to be having a spot of bother in the control room. I'm afraid they've run out of tape. It must be all the stops and starts we've had."

"Don't worry, Mr Climes," said Paddington cheerfully. "I expect you'll manage to get it right in the end."

Sunny Climes continued edging away from Paddington, and then came to a sudden halt.

"You're standing on my microphone lead," he said accusingly. Reaching forward to pick up the cable, he gave it a sharp tug.

As it happened, Paddington, ever anxious to please, beat him to it by a split second, and giving vent to a cry of alarm Sunny Climes disappeared from view round the far side of the lamppost.

"Oh dear, Mr Climes," exclaimed Paddington, hurrying to the rescue. "Are you all right?"

"No!" gurgled Sunny Climes, sounding as though a sudden typhoon had caught him in the midriff. "I am not all right! What a place to leave a shopping basket on wheels! There should be a law against people like you being allowed out by themselves."

But it was like water off a duck's back.

Paddington was already examining his basket. "You'll be pleased to know it doesn't seem to be damaged," he called. "It's still got both wheels. Hold on a minute…" His voice grew muffled as he peered inside to see if he could spot any holes in the wickerwork.

It took him a moment or two to accustom himself to the lack of light and while he was waiting he realised that Mr Climes' headphones had somehow or other fallen off inside the basket and he could hear everything that was being said outside.

Mr Climes' voice in particular came through loud and clear, and although it seemed to have lost much of its sunny quality, every word was distinct.

"I do not intend," he said, "repeat, *do not intend*, allowing myself to be beaten. These things are sent to try us, Adrian. When I started out I knew there would be days like today. In this business there are good days and there are bad days, and this one happens to be the worst day I have encountered in a very long time. I may take up playing the ukulele and become a busker."

"Worse things happen at sea," said a second voice, which Paddington recognised as belonging to the director. "It's a good job it's a recording. Just think – we might have been on air! Besides, at least we've got our sound levels sorted out."

"That's good," said Paddington, as he emerged from his basket.

He held the headphones aloft. "May I go now?"

Mr Climes, by now back on his feet, managed to summon up a hollow laugh. "If you don't mind," he said. "I've started so I'll finish."

He turned to the director. "If you have no objection, Adrian, I would like to continue where we left off."

"Good man!" exclaimed the director. "Strike while the iron's hot!" And with that he dashed back to his van.

Mr Climes took a deep breath, then he did some more counting. "Take seven," he said, after pausing to allow the director time to get back to his desk.

"Perhaps you could begin by telling us what part of the world you come from?" he said, pointing the microphone in Paddington's direction.

"Phew! Phew!" said Paddington, blowing into it as hard as he could to make sure it was working. "That's a very good question, Mr Climes. I don't really remember because I was very young at the time."

Sunny Climes permitted himself a wintery smile. "But you *must* know where it was," he said. "Everyone has some idea about where they were born."

"Not if you come from Darkest Peru," said Paddington. "It's a very big place."

"Darkest Peru!" Sunny Climes pricked up his ears. Despite everything he looked most impressed.

"Perhaps that explains your... er... lack of fundamentals.

"It must have been dark when they were dishing them out..." he added, laughing at his own joke.

Paddington gave him a hard stare. "My fundamentals are lacking!" he repeated.

Mr Climes hastily changed the subject. "It's what's known these days as being vertically challenged," he said. "Please forgive me. Er... Don't tell me you are over here to participate in the Games?"

"I won't if you would rather I didn't," said Paddington, not quite sure what the word meant.

"Aha!" said Mr Climes. "I understand." He put a finger to his nose. "Top secret, eh? Can we hold it there for a moment?"

Reaching into his pocket, he took out a sheet of paper and ran his eyes down a long list. "I can't see any mention of Darkest Peru sending a team... did you receive an official invitation to take part in the Games?"

"I don't think so," said Paddington. "I had a postcard from my Aunt Lucy the other day, but she didn't mention it."

"In short," said Mr Climes, "You are a breakaway faction going it alone. Don't worry." He put a finger to his nose again. "Your secret is safe with me.

"I must say you came round that corner at a great rate of knots. I daresay you wanted to lose some weight after all the breakfast you'd had this morning."

"No," said Paddington. "I was on my way to the bakers to get some buns. I was later than usual and I didn't want them to run out. It would have meant Mr Gruber having to wait for the second baking of the day and that would have upset his schedules."

"Gruber?" repeated Mr Climes. "Gruber? I don't know the name. Is he your trainer?"

"He has an antique shop," said Paddington. "We always have our elevenses together."

"A brilliant cover-up," said Mr Climes, hardly able to conceal his excitement.

"Tell me, what do you think of the Games so far? Are all the preparations to your liking?"

"What are they?" asked Paddington.

"What *are they*?" repeated Mr Climes. "Do you mean to say you have come all this way and you don't know what they are? This is quite extraordinary.

They're on everybody's lips."

It was Paddington's turn to edge away. "Oh dear," he said. "I hope they're not catching."

Mr Climes essayed another smile. "You're having me on," he said. "Tell me, what event do you specialise in? If I may be so bold, your legs look a bit short for the pole vault."

"My legs are a bit short for the pole vault!" repeated Paddington hotly. "But they've always been that way."

"You look as though you might be a good all-rounder," said Mr Climes soothingly.

"I expect that's because I'm wearing a duffle coat," said Paddington. "Mrs Bird says I shan't feel the benefit when I get indoors if I don't. Besides, I might catch cold."

"Sound advice for an athlete…" said Mr Climes. "Now don't tell me… let me guess… it can hardly be the long jump, or the high one come to that…"

Returning to the speed at which Paddington had come round the corner, he hazarded a guess. "A long-distance runner, perhaps?

"For instance, how long would it take you to get

from here to, say, Paddington Station?"

Paddington considered the matter for a moment or two. "I did it in just under four minutes last Sunday," he said.

"Four minutes!" exclaimed Mr Climes excitedly. "But it must be a good mile and a half from here. That has to be a world record. It's over the speed limit."

"Oh dear, is it?" said Paddington.

"The traffic lights were green all the way," he added lamely.

"I think you are hiding your light under a bushel," said Mr Climes. "Tell me, how are you on short distances – the one hundred metres for example?"

It was Paddington's turn to hazard a guess. "It depends how warm the buns are," he said, thinking about the time it took him to get from the bakers to Mr Gruber's. "On a cold day, about five seconds."

Sunny Climes was unable to contain his excitement a moment longer. "Don't forget, listeners," he shouted into the microphone, "you heard it here first!"

"Shan't be a mo…" he added, and made a dash for the green van.

Gathering his shopping basket on wheels, Paddington seized the opportunity to make good his escape.

"I'm sorry if I've kept you waiting, Mr Gruber," he said, a few minutes later.

Mr Gruber looked up from his stove at the back of the shop. "I was beginning to get worried, Mr Brown. It's unlike you to be late. The cocoa's been ready for some while."

"I met a strange man in the market," explained Paddington. "A Mr Climes... He kept me talking. I only just managed to escape when his back was turned."

"Not 'Blabbermouth' Climes!" exclaimed Mr Gruber. "I heard he was in the area. He's a famous sports writer. People hang on to his every word."

"Oh dear," said Paddington. "It sounds like him, Mr Gruber. He thinks you're my trainer for some special games." And he went on to explain all that had happened that morning to make him late.

A Chance Encounter

Mr Gruber ushered Paddington to the horsehair sofa. "If you ask me," he said, "I think it's time we had one of our chats. Mr Climes may be sunny by name, but he certainly isn't sunny by nature. Once he gets his teeth into something he never lets go."

Paddington looked up anxiously from his cocoa. "Perhaps he won't recognise me the next time we meet," he said.

"I wouldn't be too sure of that," said Mr Gruber tactfully.

"I had a disguise outfit given to me one Christmas," said Paddington. "I could wear a false beard for the time being."

"That might make matters even worse," said Mr Gruber. "If you will pardon the expression, Mr Brown, he might smell a rat. If he turns up outside my shop I suggest you hide behind this sofa while I keep him at bay. But don't forget to take your cocoa with you. Otherwise it might arouse his suspicions.

"As for the Games, I'm not surprised you haven't heard of them before. They only take place every four years and each time it is in a different country.

"People from all over the world gather together to

compete against each other in the field of sport, not just in running, but swimming and gymnastics, cycling, wrestling, weightlifting… practically everything to do with sport you can possibly think of…"

Mr Gruber had a faraway look in his eyes as he stirred his cocoa. "You may find this hard to believe, Mr Brown, but long, long ago, when I was a teenager, I achieved a certain amount of fame myself as a hurdler…"

"I always thought you were Hungarian," said Paddington, staring at his friend.

Over the years he'd never ceased to be surprised by the things Mr Gruber had done in his life, and he never once pictured him having been a teenager.

"I was a champion Hungarian hurdler," said Mr Gruber proudly. "One day I will show you some of the trophies I won."

Paddington was most impressed. "I've never won a trophy, Mr Gruber," he said. "Perhaps you could show me how it's done one day?"

Mr Gruber thought carefully before answering. "It isn't as easy as it may sound, Mr Brown," he said at last, not wishing to hurt Paddington's feelings.

"As for the Olympic Games… there isn't enough room for everyone, so only the best and the fittest are chosen to take part and for that you have to go into training a long time ahead."

Paddington looked most impressed. "I didn't know the Olympics were so important, Mr Gruber," he said.

"Just you wait," said Mr Gruber. "Soon the words will be on everyone's lips."

"That's exactly what Mr Climes said!" exclaimed Paddington.

"Well, there you are," said Mr Gruber, with a twinkle in his eye. "It must be true."

He looked at Paddington over the top of his glasses. "Having said that, I can't help thinking you were slightly over ambitious with your estimates of the time it takes you to get anywhere, Mr Brown. From here to Paddington Station in under four minutes, for example…

"It's a common mistake. People often think they are going faster than they actually are, or, worse still vice versa.

"It's no wonder Sunny Climes was excited. He's

always first with the news, even though more often than not in his haste to beat everyone else to it he manages to get hold of the wrong end of the stick. It sounds to me like one of those occasions. He must have thought he was on to a scoop.

"I suggest you keep an eye out for him during the next few days. He doesn't give up easily."

It was hard to tell whether or not Mr Gruber was being serious, but nevertheless, acting on his advice, Paddington used the back door when he left the shop.

He didn't want to run the risk of bumping into his interviewer again, and when he finally reached the safety of number thirty-two Windsor Gardens he took off his duffle coat and spent some time examining his reflection in the hall mirror.

Mr Climes was right about one thing; it did leave a lot to be desired.

"There's an item in the *Evening Banner* which may interest you, Paddington," said Mr Brown when he arrived back from the office that evening. "According to their sports reporter, Sunny Climes, there's a team from Darkest Peru arriving in this country to take part in the Olympic Games."

"Oh dear," said Paddington. "Is there?"

"I thought you would be pleased," said Mr Brown. "It doesn't say how many of them there are, and it doesn't mention any names, but the first arrival sounds pretty hot stuff… It struck me you might know who it might be."

"I think," said Paddington unhappily as he hurried upstairs to his bedroom, "you may know him already, Mr Brown."

"I wonder what he meant by that, Henry," said Mrs Brown.

"Goodness only knows," said Mr Brown. "Still waters run deep."

"There's nothing still about that bear's waters," said Mrs Bird, overhearing the conversation. "You mark my words, we haven't heard the last of it by a long chalk."

And there, for the time being at least, the matter rested.

Chapter Five

PADDINGTON IN TRAINING

ONE MORNING, SHORTLY after Paddington's chance
encounter in the Portobello Road, Mrs Brown was
pottering about in the kitchen when she happened
to glance out of the window and caught sight of
some very strange goings-on in the garden.

Wiping the steam from the glass, she took a closer
look before drawing Mrs Bird's attention to it.

"It's Paddington!" she said. "He's rolling about on the lawn like a bear possessed. I do hope he's all right."

The Browns' housekeeper joined her at the window. "Perhaps he's celebrating the fact that his sunflowers have grown so tall Mr Curry can't possibly see over the fence," she suggested.

"But they've been like that for a while now," persisted Mrs Brown.

"I must say he was unusually quiet yesterday evening," said Mrs Bird. "And he didn't finish his second mug of cocoa at breakfast, which isn't like him."

"He keeps stopping to mop his brow," said Mrs Brown. "His handkerchief looks sopping wet. I hope he isn't sickening for something."

Mrs Bird's face cleared as the penny dropped. "I do believe he's trying to do press-ups," she said. "If you want my opinion, he's got a touch of Olympic fever. There's a lot of it about at the moment and it's very catching. I even saw Mr Curry jumping up and down on the spot in his garden yesterday. I shan't be sorry when it's all over."

Mrs Brown looked relieved. "Oh, well," she said, "if that's all it is, he can't come to any great harm."

"That's as may be," said Mrs Bird darkly.

The Browns' housekeeper didn't entirely share Mrs Brown's optimism. In between the press-ups, if indeed that was what they were meant to be, Paddington wore a determined expression on his face; it was one she knew of old.

At such times there was no knowing what might be going on in his mind, although having said that, she would have been even more uneasy had she been aware of the truth.

Unbeknown to her, it had all come to a head the day before, when Paddington happened to be making his way downstairs and he came across a pamphlet on the hall mat.

There was nothing at all unusual in that. The arrival of pamphlets advertising one thing or another was a regular occurrence at number thirty-two Windsor Gardens. Hardly a day passed without the hall mat being littered with bits of paper.

Mrs Bird usually gave them short shrift. "Anyone would think this was a hotel rather than a private dwelling," was her favourite phrase as she confined whatever it was to the wastepaper bin without so much as a second glance.

Paddington had been about to do the same thing, when he caught sight of the words: FREE INTRODUCTORY OFFER! emblazoned in red across the top.

Being a bear with a keen eye for a bargain, he couldn't resist taking a closer look.

Below the headline there was a picture of a bronzed lady holding a pair of dumbbells over her head, and underneath it was another caption which read: LET ME BE YOUR PERSONAL TRAINER.

Paddington wasn't sure he wanted to go that far, but the word FREE was hard to resist, so he carried on reading.

The lady in the picture was Gladys Brimstone, late of East Acton and Rio de Janeiro, and it seemed that not only had she recently arrived in London, but she was opening a health club in the Portobello Road in time for the Olympic Games.

Dressed in singlet and shorts, her muscles rippling in the rays of the sun, she was standing on a stretch of pavement not far from Mr Gruber's shop, holding aloft a banner bearing the words: DON'T DELAY – MAKE IT TODAY.

Paddington took the pamphlet to bed with him that night and studied it carefully with the aid of his torch and a magnifying glass. According to Miss Brimstone, an hour spent with her in the gym and you were guaranteed to come out feeling a new person.

It didn't mention what effect her treatment might have on bears, but he felt sure it wouldn't be a problem because right at the end there was another banner headline saying: LARGE OR SMALL – I TREAT THEM ALL!

He felt slightly guilty about keeping the news to himself, but the pamphlet hadn't been addressed to anyone in particular. Mr Brown handed it straight back, muttering something about being late for the office, Jonathan and Judy were away at school, and try as he might, Paddington couldn't picture either Mrs Brown or Mrs Bird wanting to do press-ups on the lawn.

So it came about that shortly after his activities

in the garden, he set out on his own rather earlier than usual, hoping he would be able to investigate the matter still further before it was time for his elevenses with Mr Gruber.

As luck would have it, the door to the premises shown on the brochure was ajar, and it was with growing excitement that he pushed it open and made his way down a corridor festooned with photographs of Miss Brimstone in various poses.

It seemed as though there was no end to her talents. If she wasn't towing a steam roller uphill with the aid of rope gripped between her teeth, or canoeing down the Amazon river armed with only a bow and a quiverful of arrows, she was dressed up as Father Christmas, with one muscular arm forming a 'V' in order to crack open a walnut.

As he reached the end of the corridor, a door opened and a lady wearing hair curlers emerged.

"Good morning," she trilled. "That's what I like to see. There's nothing like getting the mail early in the morning. It's a very good start to the day."

Paddington gave her a hard stare. "I'm not a postman!" he exclaimed. "I'm Paddington Brown from Darkest Peru and I've come about your brochure."

"Oh dear," said the lady. "I do beg your pardon. You never know who does what these days."

Holding his paw in a vice-like grip, she began pumping it up and down. "Brimstone's the name. I'm not officially open as yet, but the early bird catches the worm, so I'm entirely at your disposal."

It was Paddington's turn to look confused. Close to, Miss Brimstone looked rather larger than he had expected.

"I saw the pictures in the corridor," he ventured, "and I was hoping I might have one of your walnuts. I didn't have much breakfast this morning."

Miss Brimstone gave a shudder. "A walnut for breakfast?" she boomed. "We don't have any of those goings-on round here. A glass of water and an occasional Liquorice Allsort, perhaps…"

"In that case," said Paddington. "May I have my paw back?"

Miss Brimstone promptly released her grip.

"Thank you very much," said Paddington, raising his hat politely.

Miss Brimstone gazed at the top of his head. "What on earth is that excrescence?" she exclaimed. "I've never seen anything quite like it before and I've travelled the world. Perhaps it needs a good squeeze."

Paddington anxiously ran a free paw over the top of his head. As he did so, his face cleared.

"I wouldn't do that if I were you, Miss Brimstone," he said. "It's what's left of a marmalade sandwich.

I always keep one under my hat in case I have an emergency. I had a bite out of it on the way here, just in case."

"Well, if you want me to take you on that will have to stop," said Miss Brimstone. "As of now. Snacks between meals are strictly forbidden." She eyed Paddington somewhat dubiously. "I haven't come across that kind of thing before," she said. "Even though I've been practising for over ten years."

"I'm sure you'll get it right in the end, Miss Brimstone," said Paddington politely. "My friend, Mr Gruber, is always saying 'practice makes perfect'."

Miss Brimstone gave him a sickly smile, and having locked the front door, led the way into a room at the back.

"You had better take your duffle coat off before we do anything else," she said. "Then I can give you the once-over. To start with I must take a look at your abs."

"My abs!" exclaimed Paddington. "I don't think I have any."

"Nonsense!" said Miss Brimstone briskly. "Every one has abs to a greater or lesser extent. Abs is short for abdominal muscles. Perhaps you would allow me to feel yours so that we can see where we stand…"

"If it had been a few weeks ago you could have felt my oysters," said Paddington.

"You win some – you lose some," said Miss Brimstone distantly.

Having placed his duffle coat on a nearby hook, she turned to take a closer look at her new arrival and tentatively reached out a hand.

"Tickiley wickiley," she trilled.

Paddington hastily backed away. "Bless you!" he exclaimed.

Miss Brimstone changed the subject. "It's hard to tell with all that fur," she said. "But I don't think we've left it too late. A bit off here – a bit off there, will work wonders. Tell me about your drinking habits."

"Well," said Paddington, "I usually have two mugs of cocoa at breakfast, and then another one for my elevenses."

"That's something else that will have to stop," said Miss Brimstone sternly. "Cocoa is far too rich. A glass or two of hot water will be much better for you in the long run."

She led him towards some scales.

"I think perhaps we had better check our weight first of all…"

"After you, Miss Brimstone," said Paddington politely.

"No," said Miss Brimstone through slightly gritted teeth. "After *you*. When I said *our* weight I meant yours, of course.

"Tell me, do you get much exercise?"

"I ran all the way down to the Portobello Road the other day," said Paddington, "I was going so fast I was asked to do an interview on the radio."

"Good… good," said Miss Grimshaw. "Bully for you! What did you do then?"

"After I finished the interview," said Paddington,

"I called in at the bakers. I have a standing order for buns, and while I was doing that, Mr Gruber made some cocoa. Then we sat down on the horsehair sofa at the back of his shop and had our elevenses together. We do that most days."

"Tut, tut," said Miss Brimstone. "That's something else that will have to stop."

She gave Paddington's stomach a sharp poke.

"Your waistline needs trimming. Too many French fries I would say, at a guess. We can soon burn that off…"

"Burn it off!" exclaimed Paddington in alarm.

"It's a technical term," said Miss Brimstone hastily. "There's no cause for alarm. We have our methods. It's a case of being cruel to be kind.

"First of all, repeat after me – *I hate French fries.*"

"I'm afraid I can't do that," said Paddington firmly.

"Why ever not?" asked Miss Brimstone.

"Because my Aunt Lucy brought me up never to tell lies," said Paddington.

Miss Brimstone hastily changed the subject.

"The thing is," she said, "you can either sweat your excess weight off by coming here several days a week for six months, in which case all you need do is sign on the dotted line if you want to pay by standing order, or you can go for my all-in-one crash course. The choice is yours."

Leading Paddington across the room, she pointed towards some parallel bars on the wall.

"Perhaps we should start with an agility test.

"First of all, put your right leg up and rest it on the bottom bar."

Paddington eyed it doubtfully. "I'm afraid it's a bit high," he said.

"Now, we mustn't be defeatist, must we," said Miss Brimstone. "Take a deep, deep breath and try a little harder...

"A teensy bit more..."

Paddington began waving his paws wildly in the air for fear he might lose his balance.

"More... more... more..." urged Miss Brimstone.

"Brilliant!" she cried, as Paddington managed to touch the bar with his toes at long last. "Top hole! I knew you would get there in the end.

"Now try the other leg."

There was a crash as Paddington landed on the

floor with both legs in the air.

Miss Brimstone gazed down at him. "Oh dear," she said. "I was rather expecting you to remove your right leg first.

"Bravo, though!" she continued, "You have taken up the scissors position. None of my other clients have ever managed that the first time round."

Paddington attempted to unwind himself as best he could. He wasn't familiar with the scissors position. It felt more like one of Mr Brown's corkscrews to him and after a moment or two he gave up the struggle and remained where he had landed.

"Was that it?" he gasped.

"Was what what?" asked Miss Brimstone.

"The crash course," said Paddington.

Miss Brimstone gave him another sickly smile. "Certainly not!" she said. "Whatever next?" She pointed towards the back of the gym. "There's a whole lot more to come… the rowing machine… the treadmill… we mustn't rest on our laurels, must we."

"I don't mind, Miss Brimstone," said Paddington. "Except it doesn't feel like laurels. It's more like the floor, and it's very hard."

"These things are all in the mind," said Miss Brimstone.

"Is anything the matter?" she asked, proffering a helping hand. "You look rather disappointed about something."

Paddington gazed up at her. He was very conscious of the fact that her tattoos seemed to have taken on a life of their own. Some of them were making very odd faces indeed, mostly in his direction.

"I was hoping you might lift me up with your

teeth," he said. "Like you do in your brochure."

"It just so happens I have a bad back," said Miss Brimstone stiffly.

"I expect it's all those steam rollers you've been pulling," said Paddington.

Miss Brimstone chose not to answer.

"Now, on the subject of snacks," she said. "If you take doughnuts, for example… a typical sugar-coated doughnut contains over 200 calories."

"It sounds very good value, Miss Brimstone," said Paddington, raising his hat politely as he rose to his feet. "If I may, I wouldn't mind two of those while I recover."

"You will do no such thing," barked Miss Brimstone sternly. "You must realise that in order to counterbalance the gain in weight from eating just one doughnut you would need to spend nearly an hour on a bicycle."

"That's all right," said Paddington, breathing a sigh of relief.

"You don't mind doing that?"

"I haven't got a bicycle," said Paddington.

"Aha!" said Miss Brimstone. "In that case, we

are in luck's way. I happen to have the very thing." She pointed to a contraption in the corner of her gym. "It's what is known as an exercise machine."

Paddington eyed the object dubiously.

"I don't think Mr Brown will be very keen on having one of those in our driveway," he said. "He won't be able to get his car out for a start."

"Don't worry," said Miss Brimstone. "It's bolted to the floor.

"You may find this hard to believe," she continued, "but some of my clients spend an hour working out in the gym and at the end of it all they go straight to the nearest cake shop and undo all the good work by stuffing themselves with blueberry muffins. Some of the larger ones contain nearly 400 calories."

Paddington didn't find it hard to believe at all. All the talk about food you ought not to eat was occupying his own mind to the exclusion of everything else, and he was beginning to feel hungrier than ever.

"We never had anything like that in Darkest Peru," he said, looking at the machine.

"Have no fear," said Miss Brimstone. "It doesn't go anywhere. That's the beauty of it. You simply pedal away to your heart's content for as long as it takes to remove the excess fat. Allow me to give you a hand…"

Having managed to lift Paddington on to the saddle, she stood back and surveyed the result.

"Oh dear," she said. "Our feet *are* rather a long way from the pedals…"

"I'm afraid I can't reach the handlebars either," said Paddington.

"Stay right where you are," said Miss Brimstone. "Don't move an inch or we could have a nasty ax. I shall have to try lowering the saddle. Excuse me while I look for a suitable spanner."

Reaching for her handbag she began rummaging through it. "It's a shame," she said. "My treatment is guaranteed to take you out of yourself."

"I think I'd rather stay inside it for the time being if you don't mind, Miss Brimstone," said Paddington.

Marooned in midair, he clung on to the saddle with one paw as Miss Brimstone handed him a card. "It's a list of my charges," she said briefly. "You may like to browse through them while you're waiting."

Paddington did as he was told and then wished he hadn't.

"It's a lot of buns' worth," he announced over the sound of banging coming from the direction of the front door. "I shall have to think it over."

"Oh dear," said Miss Brimstone, abandoning her search for a spanner. "It really isn't your fault, but I shouldn't have taken you on in the first place. I shan't be ready for a day or two and now it sounds as though I have another customer…"

Seeing what she took to be a look of disappointment on Paddington's face, and conscious of the continued banging, Miss Brimstone lifted him off the saddle.

"At least you can take a present away with you!" she said. "I know you will want to come back when you've thought things over, so in the meantime, if I can have your name, I would like to present you with a special gift voucher." She scribbled a note on one of her cards. "It allows for one free go on my Advanced Personal Training Course. In the meantime you can tell all your friends what a splendid time you've had."

As she was ushering Paddington towards the front door the banging stopped and whoever was outside pushed open the letter box flap.

Anxious to be of help, Paddington made a dash for the door and held the flap open with one paw while he peered through the gap.

"Bear!" bellowed a familiar voice. "I might have known! What are you up to in there?"

In a state of shock, Paddington let go of the flap and as it sprang back into place there was a cry of a pain from outside.

"Oh dear," said Miss Brimstone. She slid back the door bolt. "Was that a friend of yours?"

"Not really," said Paddington. "It's Mr Curry. Mrs Bird says he's always sticking his nose into things that don't concern him."

"It sounds as though he's done it once too often," said Miss Brimstone. "And I haven't even unpacked my first aid box yet."

"Are you practising for the Games, Mr Curry?" asked Paddington hopefully, as he went outside and found the Browns' neighbour dancing up and down on the pavement.

"No I am not, bear!" barked the Browns' neighbour, rubbing his nose. "You know very well what happened."

"I'm sorry, Mr Curry," said Paddington. "I didn't realise it was your nose. I thought it was someone trying to deliver a parcel…"

"Are you trying to tell me you mistook my nose for a parcel?" bellowed Mr Curry. "Just you wait until I get back home. I shall report you for this."

"Oh dear," said Miss Brimstone. "Have a nice day!" With that, she handed Paddington the card she had been carrying and hastily shut the door, ramming the bolt home for good measure.

"What have you got there, bear?" demanded Mr Curry.

"It's a prize," said Paddington. "Were you going to take one of the courses?"

"Take one of the courses?" repeated Mr Curry. He pointed to a board on the wall. "Have you seen the prices? It's disgraceful. I was about to complain.

"Er… what sort of prize did you win?" he asked casually.

A gleam came into Mr Curry's eyes when Paddington told him. "If you let me have that card, bear," he said, "I promise we'll hear no more about your deliberate attack on my proboscis. Keep it for yourself, and who knows what might happen?

"And no telling anyone else," he warned. "Otherwise it will be the worse for you."

With that, he put the card into his wallet and went on his way in high good humour.

Paddington kept to his side of the bargain and didn't mention what had happened to anyone, but

Mr Curry couldn't wait to tell everyone else he met about his windfall, without mentioning how it had come about, of course.

The news spread like wildfire, and many a curtain twitched in Windsor Gardens a few days later when he set off early in the morning for Miss Brimstone's gymnasium.

They twitched again when he staggered back home later that day, cutting a sorry figure in his bedraggled shorts and sweat-stained shirt. For some reason he kept shaking his fist towards number thirty-two Windsor Gardens, but wisely Mrs Brown pretended there was no one at home.

It was Mrs Bird who

eventually discovered the truth. "I thought it was unlike Mr Curry to splash out on a course like that," she said. "It seems he had a free pass, but it turned out to be in someone else's name so he wasn't able to use it."

"I wonder how he came by it in the first place?" said Mrs Brown.

"I wonder," said Mrs Bird. "But I haven't seen Paddington doing his press-ups on the lawn for several days. I think he's keeping a low profile."

It was left for Mr Gruber to sum things up.

"I do like stories with a happy ending, Mr Brown," he said, when Paddington had finished telling him the truth of the matter.

"That dreadful Mr Curry won't be bullying you again for a long time. Miss Brimstone has got her business off to a flying start, and here we are again, enjoying our elevenses in peace.

"Everything in moderation," he said. "That's my motto. Not too little; and not too much. That being so, what is this life if you can't enjoy your elevenses undisturbed?"

There was no answer to that so, having considered the matter carefully, Paddington helped himself to another bun.

"Perhaps I might leave cutting down and having one less until tomorrow, Mr Gruber," he said.

"That sounds a very good idea," said Mr Gruber. "I think I will join you."

Chapter Six

PADDINGTON FLIES A KITE

IF IT HADN'T been for the fact that apart from a slight breeze it was a particularly warm July morning, Paddington might not have stopped on his way to the market in order to bathe his feet. But the plastic padding pool of crystal clear water with chunks of ice floating in it was hard to resist. It seemed a very good start to the day. So when a man behind a makeshift counter invited him to make use of it he accepted the invitation without so much as a second thought.

Time passes very quickly when you are having fun, but it felt like only a moment or two before he heard a voice calling out to him.

He stared at the man behind the counter. "I owe you ten pounds!" he repeated hotly. "But I've only just got here."

"You've 'ad your feet in the water for a good ten minutes," said the man. "And it's a pound a minute."

"A pound a minute?" uttered Paddington. He could hardly believe his ears.

"It's coming up to eleven now," said the man.

"Eleven!" repeated Paddington in alarm.

"You 'eard," said the man crossly. "What are you? Some kind of tame parrot... repeating everything I say?"

"But I've only got ten pence," said Paddington. "And that has to last me until the end of the week."

"Ten pence!" echoed the man. "Did I 'ear you say you've only got ten pence?"

"Now you're doing it," said Paddington.

"Doing what?" said the man.

"Repeating what I just said," exclaimed Paddington. He raised his hat politely. "I think it must be catching. I was on my way to see Mr Gruber when you asked me if I would like to bathe my feet. It's a hot day, so it felt like a good idea, and..."

"Thirteen and counting," broke in the man, looking at his watch. "I was assuming," he continued, choosing his words with care, "that you'd read the sign over the pool before you took the plunge. It's all there in black and white. Now I've got a good idea. I suggest you take your feet out of that water in double-quick time and 'op it. My fish are 'aving enough trouble as it is – threshing to and fro like they don't know if they're coming or going."

Hearing the word 'fish', Paddington scrambled out of the blue plastic paddling pool as fast as he could and peered down at the water for the first time. Sure enough, a shoal of tiny black creatures were circling round and round in the very spot where he had just been standing.

"I wish I'd brought my fishing net with me," he said.

"That would have been all I need," said the man. "I've only just taken delivery of them *garra rufas*. Very valuable, they are. They're from the other side of the world and they've got no teeth."

"Oh dear," said Paddington. "I should ask for your money back if I were you."

"But that's the whole point," said the man. "They don't bite, they suck. It's the latest thing in what is known as the world of fish pedicure. Which is a fancy name for what is the same as manicuring fingers only it 'as to do with the feet. Them fish remove the dead skin from between people's toes without damaging the 'ealthy skin underneath it like there's no tomorrow. If you ask me they must have been 'aving trouble with your follicles."

"My follicles!" repeated Paddington. "I'd better tell Mrs Bird."

"Oh dear," said the man. "'Ere we go again. Follicles," he explained, "are the sunken bits you 'as between your toes. Bears' follicles must be deeper than other people's. I expect the fish 'ad trouble getting their little 'eads inside. Must be very frustrating. I bet some of them wished they'd been born with teeth after all."

Glancing up, the salesman's face suddenly cleared as he realised a small crowd had collected while they had been talking.

"Roll up, roll up," he called, hastily changing his tune.

"Gather round everybody. This young bear gentlemen 'ere is what's known as a trendsetter. Or he would 'ave been, except he's 'aving trouble with 'is follicles.

"For that very reason I'm not charging him anything," he added, giving Paddington a nudge, "and since I know 'e's in an 'urry to be on 'is way, I suggest you form an orderly queue. . ."

As the crowd set about following the man's instructions, Paddington took the hint and made good his escape.

Leaving a trail of wet footprints behind him, he hurried down the Portobello Road as fast as he could in order to tell Mr Gruber about his latest adventure.

"I sometimes think people see you coming, Mr Brown," said his friend, as he busied himself getting the cocoa ready for their elevenses, while Paddington dealt with the buns. "Things do seem to happen when you're out and about."

"It's a bit early in the day too," said Paddington. "It's only just past eleven o'clock."

A thoughtful look came over Mr Gruber's face as

he settled himself down on the horsehair sofa at the back of the shop. "This hot weather isn't good news when you're trying to run a business," he mused. "People want to be out and about, not stuck inside an antique shop. I had been toying with the idea of putting our deck chairs out on the pavement like we used to, but all this talk of dipping your feet into ice-cold water has given me an idea."

He paused. "Seeing Jonathan and Judy are home for the summer holidays, perhaps you had better see what they feel about it first of all, but I think a nice peaceful picnic in the park this afternoon will do us all the world of good."

"A picnic in the park!" exclaimed Judy, when Paddington rushed home to tell the others. "What a lovely idea. Trust Mr Gruber to invite us along too." She got up off the lawn and brushed herself down. "I'd better make some sandwiches."

"May I help," asked Paddington excitedly. "Bears are good at sandwiches."

Jonathan licked a forefinger and held it over his head. "There's a nice breeze," he announced. "I might take my kite. I haven't flown it for years."

He rushed upstairs and returned a moment or so later armed with a multicoloured object almost as tall as Paddington.

"It's what's known as a double butterfly kite," he said. "The frame is made of balsawood and the rest of it is Japanese tissue paper. I made it myself," he added proudly. "*And* I painted it!"

"I expect bears would be good at flying kites," said Paddington hopefully.

Jonathan eyed him dubiously. "We'll see," he replied vaguely. "It isn't always as easy as it might sound."

"You wouldn't want to be carried off by the wind," said Judy, coming to her brother's rescue.

"There's no knowing where you might end up," agreed Jonathan gratefully.

Both Mrs Bird and Mrs Brown were only too pleased to have the house to themselves, so Mr Gruber's suggestion met with all-round approval, and it was a happy party that eventually set off early that afternoon.

Paddington gazed around with interest as they entered the park. There were all manner of things going on. To start with there was a children's playground full of climbing frames, which looked very tempting. Then there were several outdoor restaurants; but best of all, there was a large lake with boats on it, so he made a beeline for that.

"I think I might test my follicles first of all," he announced, as he dipped his toes into the water.

But once again it seemed as though it wasn't meant to be, for his feet had hardly entered the water before a man in uniform emerged from behind a bush.

"What's all this going on?" he asked severely. "Can't you read?"

He pointed to a nearby sign emblazoned with the words: NO BATHING, FISHING OR DOGS ALLOWED IN THIS WATER in large letters.

"It doesn't say anything about bears," protested Judy, coming to Paddington's rescue. "Or dipping your feet in the water, come to that."

"That's as may be," said the man. "But it has to do with Health and Safety. Health on account of the fact that we don't know where that young bear's feet have been, and safety on account of the fact that some of the fish around here have got very sharp teeth and they might fancy partaking of a toe or two for their afternoon tea."

Paddington hastily withdrew his feet from the water just as there was a splash of something breaking the surface nearby.

"See what I mean," said the man. "That was a narrow squeak if ever there was one. Probably a passing pike with an eye on your digits."

He glanced at Jonathan's kite. "And the same applies to that contraption," he said. "There's a time and place for everything. What goes up must come down. And when that happens it might land on someone's head.

"If I were you," he added, not unkindly. "I'd take it somewhere quiet where you can't be seen."

"Oh dear," said Mr Gruber, as the inspector turned on his heels and went on his way. "That wasn't a very good start."

"Don't worry, Mr Gruber," said Judy. "No matter what, they can't stop us from having our sandwiches."

"I know a good place for a picnic," broke in Jonathan. "It's where I used to go when I was small. Follow me…" And without further ado he led the way round the lake.

"We must be getting near the Open Air Theatre," said Judy, when they reached the far side.

Paddington pricked up his ears. "I've never heard of a theatre in the open air before," he said.

Jonathan pointed towards a poster. "Well, there you are," he said. "They're doing *Hamlet* today. The wind's blowing the right way, so with a bit of luck you might be able to hear some of it."

Paddington licked his lips. Privately, he thought Hamlet sounded like a small ham sandwich, but he didn't let on. "What is it about?" he asked.

"Most of the play takes place in a castle called Elsinore," said Jonathan. "And it's very bloodthirsty. Hamlet's father was King of Denmark and when he slew the King of Norway, his son vowed to avenge him."

"Meanwhile," said Judy, "Hamlet's mother, Gertrude, marries someone called Claudius, who is none other than the brother of Hamlet's father."

"Then," said Mr Gruber, "Hamlet's father appears as a ghost and tells his son that he was in fact murdered by Claudius... and he must take his revenge."

"It sounds very complicated," said Paddington.

"That's only the beginning," said Jonathan. "There's someone called Polonius, who is always in the way, so he has to go..."

"And then there's Polonius' daughter, Ophelia," said Judy. "She's keen on Hamlet, but after he says, 'Get thee to a nunnery', she ends up drowning herself."

"Don't forget Yorick," broke in Mr Gruber. "He gets killed by mistake. Hamlet has a lot to say about that when some grave diggers come across his skull and give it to him."

Jonathan struck a pose. "Alas, poor Yorick," he proclaimed. "I knew him well..."

It struck Paddington that there couldn't be many people left by the end.

Mr Gruber laughed. "You are quite right, Mr Brown," he said. "And those who are still alive don't fare too well. Ophelia's brother, Laertes, gets killed in a sword fight with Hamlet, and at the end even Hamlet himself falls foul of a poisoned sword."

"It's really a play about a man who couldn't make up his mind," explained Judy. "'To be or not to be' is one of Hamlet's great lines. Actors often milk it for all it's worth and make it last for ever."

"When we were doing it as our end of term play last year, someone called out, 'Hurry up, I've got a train to catch'," said Jonathan. "It didn't half get a laugh."

"I don't think you ought to tell Paddington things like that," whispered Judy. "He takes these things so seriously. Remember the very first time he went to the theatre and got terribly upset when Sir Sealy Bloom threw his daughter out of the house. He went round to his dressing room during the interval and complained."

"Not much chance of that happening today," said Jonathan cheerfully.

He led the way round to the back of the theatre

where there was a large area of grass, most of which had been worn away through lack of rain. A few deck chairs stood abandoned, but there wasn't a soul in sight, and apart from a distant sound of voices they might have been on a desert island.

"It's often like this once everyone has gone in to see the show," said Jonathan knowledgeably. "The great thing is, if there is any wind at all, the theatre itself helps to deflect it upwards, so it's ideal for flying a kite."

And while Mr Gruber and Judy set about arranging the deck chairs and getting ready for the picnic, he led Paddington towards the far end in order to explain the ins and outs of it all.

"This shape of kite is particularly good," he explained. "Even if I say so myself. On a good day it's almost as though it has a life of its own; something inside it that makes it want to fly.

"It really needs two people, of course," he continued, handing Paddington a reel of string attached to the kite so that he could get the feel of it. "Whoever is flying it holds the reel in one hand and lets the string slide through the fingers of the other hand as it takes off. In that way they can stay in control by giving a tug every now and then to make the kite fly higher still. In your case, of course, you would have to do it all by paw.

"The assistant – that's me in this case – lifts the kite gently into the air and stands with his or her back to the wind, like so… while they wait for an upward rush of air which lifts it out of their hand and…"

"Watch out!" cried Paddington. "Stay where you are. I'm coming through!"

There was pounding of feet as he shot past Jonathan and disappeared in a cloud of dust.

"Did you see that?" cried Jonathan, turning to the others. "Did you see it? It only took one small puff."

"He did say bears might be good at flying a kite," said Judy. "But that's something else again." She hesitated. "He was going so fast I lost sight of him."

Mr Gruber coughed. "I have a feeling Mr Brown went round the corner near the theatre by mistake," he said.

"That's torn it," groaned Jonathan, as they made their way back towards the entrance and there was neither sight nor sound of Paddington.

"Where can he be?" said Judy.

"If my kite's caught up in a tree and they're in the middle of *Hamlet* I shall never get it back," moaned Jonathan. "The play goes on for ever. There are five acts."

Mr Gruber paused for a moment and put a hand to his ear. "It may not be as bad as you think," he said. "It sounds to me as though it's the beginning of Act Three. The important bit Judy was talking about, where Hamlet can't make up his mind what to do next. Listen…"

"To be…" proclaimed a voice in sonorous tones. There was a long pause, then came the words, "…or not to be…"

"Make up your mind," shouted a familiar voice from somewhere overhead."I've got a train to catch."

A gasp went round the audience. It was followed almost immediately by a mixture of scattered applause and catcalls.

A woman's voice could be heard shouting, "Shame!"

The immediate response, "Get thee to a nunnery…" was greeted by a loud cheer.

Mr Gruber pointed to a dark shape in the foliage high above the back of the stage.

"That looks like Mr Brown," he said.

It was hard to tell what came next because of the noise from the audience that followed every line of dialogue, but eventually things settled down and there was a shower of leaves as Paddington began his descent.

Judy closed her eyes as the branches began to sway more and more. "I can't watch," she said. "Suppose one of his duffle coat toggles gets caught in something?"

"I shouldn't worry," said Mr Gruber. "Climbing trees is another thing bears are good at. Mr Brown must have done a lot of it when he was a cub."

As things turned out, they had rather longer to wait than expected, but eventually he emerged from behind the trees armed with the kite.

"I'm sorry to be such a long time," he said, as he handed it back to Jonathan. "But I think I know who did it…"

"Did what?" chorused Jonathan and Judy.

"Killed Mr Yorick," said Paddington. "I had a good view of the stage from where I was sitting and I saw a man putting someone's skull on to a table. I've phoned the police with a description."

"You've done *what*?" exclaimed Judy.

"Well," said Paddington. "I didn't exactly do it myself, but I met the inspector who told me off for putting my feet in the water. I think he must have followed us here. He told me to stay where I was and he would do it for me.

"Then someone from the theatre came along and wanted to see my ticket. When I said I didn't have one, he showed me the exit. So here I am."

Mr Gruber glanced at the others. It was rather a lot to take in at one go.

"Can you hear what I can hear?" he asked, as the sound of a distant siren rose above the voices on the stage. "It may not be heading our way, but I suggest we beat a hasty retreat, just in case. We can eat our sandwiches on the way.

"It seemed a good idea at the time," he added, as they made their way towards the exit, "but better safe than sorry." He nodded towards Paddington. "I think it's turned out to be one of those days. These things happen from time to time."

"It's a pity they don't have tree climbing in the Olympics," said Jonathan. "He was up and down it like a yo-yo."

"It would have been worth a gold medal for sure," agreed Judy.

"I don't think I shall ever be fit enough to go and

see the Games," said Paddington sadly. "Let alone take part in them."

"You don't have to be fit if you're a spectator," explained Mr Gruber. "It only applies to the athletes who are taking part."

"I didn't know that," said Paddington, looking most aggrieved. "You'd think they would tell people these things."

"Anyway," broke in Jonathan. "You can sit at home and watch them on television."

"People will have their eyes glued to the screen," said Judy.

"It sounds a bit painful to me," said Paddington. "I think I might have another sandwich. I feel better already."

"I can't wait to read the reviews in tomorrow's papers," said Mr Brown, later that day, when Jonathan and Judy related the tale of their adventure in the park. "There have been a good many versions of *Hamlet* staged over the years, but it sounds as if this one beats them all."

"The trouble is, anyone who goes to see it after

reading the reviews will be in for a disappointment," said Mrs Brown. "There won't be any 'noises off '."

Mrs Bird kept her counsel. Something about the way Paddington was behaving caused her to wonder if he might be sickening for something. He was unusually quiet over dinner and it wasn't long after they had finished before he disappeared upstairs. He didn't even wait to see if there was a second helping.

Later on that evening, as she followed suit, she noticed a chink of light under his bedroom door so, having knocked on it and received no reply, she tiptoed in.

Everything seemed to be in order. His duffle coat and hat were in their usual place on the back of the door. The framed photograph of Aunt Lucy was on the bedside table, but there was no sign of Paddington himself, although as she went further into the room she realised there was a curious lump in the middle of the bed.

As she drew near she gave a cough and a small figure emerged from under the duvet.

"Do you believe in ghosts, Mrs Bird?" asked Paddington.

"Well," said Mrs Bird carefully. "I can't say I have ever actually seen one myself."

"I've been thinking," said Paddington sleepily. "I wouldn't like to live in Elsinore. It must be full of ghosts."

"Elsinore is in Denmark," said Mrs Bird gravely. "Which is a very long way away. I shouldn't lose any sleep over it."

"I'm glad of that," said Paddington. He lay back on his pillow and drew the duvet up round his chin.

"Mind you," continued Mrs Bird. "I daresay there are good ghosts as well as bad ones. There are certain beings on this earth who make such a deep impression while they are around you feel they will always be somewhere around, watching over us. It isn't quite the same thing as being a ghost, of course, but it's very comforting."

She didn't add that she was looking at one such being right now, but by then Paddington was already fast asleep, so having made sure the sheets were well and truly tucked in, she crept quietly off to bed herself.

Tomorrow was another day, and with a bear about the house there was no knowing what might happen next, so it was as well to be prepared.

Chapter Seven

PADDINGTON ON TRACK

IT WAS A few mornings later when Mrs Brown happened to glance out of the downstairs window of number thirty-two Windsor Gardens and she was taken aback to see a group of men behaving very strangely in their front garden.

Two of them were struggling with a large concrete plant pot, while a third, having made a frame with the forefinger and thumb of both hands, peered at them through the opening. For some reason it seemed to be giving him a great deal of pleasure.

She had intended checking the weather before she went shopping, but instead she called out to Mrs Bird.

"Come quickly!" she cried. "There are some men moving Henry's begonias. That old concrete pot of his is already cracked. If it gets any worse and breaks in half, we shall never hear the last of it."

Even as she spoke there was a momentary flash as the third man recorded the scene on a digital camera.

"Leave it to me," called Mrs Bird grimly.

Pausing only to arm herself with a suitable weapon from the hall stand, she flung open the front door and confronted the intruders.

Although she didn't actually shout '*en garde*', her sudden appearance brandishing a rolled umbrella had the desired effect. The men froze in their tracks.

"Dear lady," said the man with the camera nervously. "Please don't be alarmed. It's only a recce." He held out his hand. "Mervyn's the name. I'm the designer. The thing is, if the director likes the look of your house we may need to rearrange things a bit before we start filming…"

"Filming?" repeated Mrs Bird, taking a firmer grip of her umbrella. "What do you mean, filming?"

"Don't tell me you haven't been warned!" exclaimed Mervyn. "This is unforgivable. Hang on a moment; I'll contact Head Office straight away.

"Drop everything!" he called to the others.

"Don't you dare!" broke in Mrs Bird. "If anything happens to those begonias I shall hold you responsible."

Hastily producing a mobile phone, Mervyn began dialling a number.

"I'm afraid there's been a bit of a breakdown in communications," he said, over his shoulder. "But take my word for it, you won't recognise your house after we've finished, and you'll be thanking us for it. If we don't change the layout people will be ringing your door bell at all hours. Some don't take no for an answer and that can be very tedious. We'll paint the front door a different colour for the time being," he continued, "but…"

He broke off as a fourth figure dressed from head to toe in white: white suit, white shirt and tie, white shoes, floated in through the front drive. The only concession to colour was a single blue peacock's feather stuck at a rakish angle in the band of his broad-brimmed, white hat.

"Ah," said Mervyn. "Here comes Fernando. He'll sort things out."

The newcomer came to a halt before reaching them, and having formed a similar frame to Mervyn's with his fingers, gazed intently through it as he pirouetted in a half-circle on one foot, and took in the situation at a glance.

"It must be meant," he said, addressing Mrs Bird.

"I see you ina da part of the Fairy Princess. Unfurling your parasol and floating off into the sunset – just lika da Mary Poppins. Light as a feather, only much prettier of course. I kiss your hand in anticipation, *señorita*."

"*Señora!*" said Mrs Bird firmly.

"I should be so lucky!" said Fernando. Taking her free hand in his, he raised it to his lips before turning to the designer. "Ringa da central casting, before isa too late."

"I think you had better come inside," said Mrs Bird weakly.

"Any chance of putting this pot down, mum?" called one of the men.

"If you promise to do it very carefully," replied Mrs Bird dreamily.

Fernando and Mervyn followed her into the hall at the same moment as Mrs Brown emerged from the front room.

"What is going on?" she said. "Whatever it may be, it isn't convenient. I'm about to go shopping."

"And so you shall, *señora*," said Fernando, having first made sure she was wearing a wedding ring. "So you shall. Please do not let us detain you a moment longer."

"The last thing we would wish is to cause you any inconvenience," agreed Mervyn. "Provided you use the back entrance for the time being, you can come and go whenever you please. But if you could be a darling and keep your voice down, that would be wonderful."

"In the meantime…" Fernando produced a folded sheet of paper from an inside pocket and handed it to Mrs Brown, along with a crumpled piece of newspaper. "Here, *señora*, are our credentials."

"Home for Retired Bears..." began Mrs Brown, reading from the heading on the notepaper. She held it up for Mrs Bird to see. "I do believe it's from Paddington's Aunt Lucy..."

But Mrs Bird had already caught sight of a familiar face in the piece of newspaper. "It's that dreadful Sunny Climes!" she said. "It must be a cutting from the *Evening Banner*. If you remember, I said at the time we hadn't heard the last of him."

"Oh dear," said Mrs Brown. "I wonder how it reached Peru?"

"Bad news travels," said Mrs Bird.

She turned to Fernando. "If it's Paddington you want to see, he's upstairs. It's the end of the month, so he's probably doing his accounts. If that's the case, I would rather you didn't disturb him. Stopping halfway through the adding up might well mean his having to start all over again."

"A person of such importance," said Fernando, "and he is doing his own accounts?" Clearly, it was a concept he had never encountered before.

"Whatever next? Besides, it is not what you might calla da higher mathematics."

"It is if you happen to be a bear," said Mrs Brown.

Mrs Bird read the look on her face. "You carry on with your shopping," she said. "I'll deal with this."

"I have come a longa da way," persisted Fernando. "In Peru, his fame as an athlete has spread lika da wildfire. Isa da talking point wherever you go."

"That's as may be," said Mrs Bird. "But may I suggest you tell us exactly what it is you want to see him about."

Fernando reached out for her hand again and clasped it in his. "I have been commissioned, *señora*," he said grandly, "to make a film of his exploits. At alla da costs they must be preserved for posterity.

"Perhaps, if *Señor* Paddington is engaged, I will telephone his manager and make an appointment?"

Mrs Brown let go of her shopping bag. "I think I had better stay after all," she said.

"Do you both take milk?" asked Mrs Bird. "I'll put the coffee on."

*

To say the Brown family were rocked to their very foundations by the news that Paddington was about to star in a film, would have been putting it mildly.

Fernando spent some time in the kitchen with Mrs Bird explaining matters, while Mervyn devoted his time to Mrs Brown, Jonathan and Judy, and latterly Paddington himself when he came downstairs to see what was going on.

Long after Fernando and Mervyn had departed in search of a suitable location for what they called the 'nitty-gritty', and Paddington had gone back upstairs to write a postcard to his Aunt Lucy, the rest of the family talked of little else.

"What *are* we going to do?" said Mrs Brown.

"If that bear's going to be in a film," said Mrs Bird, "his duffle coat had better go to the dry-cleaners. If I take it first thing tomorrow morning he'll get it back the same day."

"He won't like it," said Judy. "He's very fond of his stains. Each one tells a story."

"I can't help that," said Mrs Bird firmly. "Needs must."

The discussion carried on through lunch and

continued until the evening, when Mr Brown arrived home from the office.

"Has anyone ever wondered how the Home for Retired Bears came into being?" asked Mrs Bird.

"I can't say it's kept me awake at night," said Mr Brown. "I've always assumed it had something to do with the Lima Borough Council."

"It's a fascinating story," continued Mrs Bird. "*Señor* Fernando told me all about it. Apparently it dates back to the time when the Peruvians were building a huge boat on Lake Titicaca."

"The *Yavari*," broke in Jonathan. "We've been learning about it at school. All 210 tonnes were shipped to Peru as a kit of parts. Most were made in Birmingham, but the sections for the hull were made in London by a firm called Thames Ironworks and Shipbuilding, who also founded West Ham Football Club. Which is how they came to be nicknamed 'The Hammers', because of all the hammering of the iron plates that went on at the time."

"I was beginning to wonder how you remembered all that," said Judy. "I might have known it had something to do with football."

Jonathan gave her an aggrieved look. "It wasn't just that," he said. "Our geography master has got pictures of all the problems they had transporting everything.

"Lake Titicaca is 12,500 feet above sea level, and for the last 350 kilometres it all had to be loaded on to mules. They could only cope with a small amount at a time."

"I don't see why they needed to have a boat that size up there in the first place," said Judy.

"It's like the old joke," explained Jonathan. "Why did the chicken cross the road? Answer: To get to the other side. Lake Titicaca is the biggest landlocked stretch of water in South America. It's like an inland sea and there was no other means of communication in those days."

"Anyway," broke in Mrs Bird, unable to contain herself a moment longer, "going back to the Home for Retired Bears. Apparently the whole operation took years rather than months to complete, and a rich English industrialist who happened to be exploring Peru at the time was so mortified at the way bears were being uprooted from their natural habitat, he took pity on them and set up a trust fund. At the same time he purchased a large property in Lima to take care of the older ones who had nowhere to go."

"What a kind thought," said Mrs Brown. "Is he still around?"

Mrs Bird shook her head. "It all took place well over 150 years ago. But before he died he made sure everything was taken care of. The occupants live rent-free, but they are expected to work for their living and in fact they have quite a steady income from all the things they make.

"In the winter they are very industrious. They make marmalade, knit sweaters and scarves, and make all kinds of other ethnic items. Then, during the summer months when the tourists arrive, they set up their stands in the market. They are said to drive a hard bargain."

"That bit sounds familiar," said Mr Brown.

"According to Fernando, provided he doesn't go too much over budget, financing the film isn't a problem."

"Well I never," said Mrs Brown. "I have often wondered how it all came about."

"Such a charming man," said Mrs Bird, bringing the conversation to an end as she went out into the kitchen. "A joy to be with."

"I think she's got the hots for him," whispered Judy.

"What a dreadful expression," said Mrs Brown.

"You don't think, Mary…" began Mr Brown. "I mean, one thing leads to another…"

"The grass is always greener on the other side of the fence," said Mrs Brown. "You should know that, Henry, and Mrs Bird certainly does."

The possibility of losing both Paddington and Mrs Bird into the bargain was too awful to contemplate, so she hastily changed the subject.

"It's a big upheaval," said Mr Brown. "It could go on for weeks. I hope we're getting paid for it."

"*Señor* Fernando told Mrs Bird he is offering his services for a da love," said Jonathan. "Except for the travelling expenses."

"So shall we, won't we, Henry?" said Mrs Brown.

"I, er…" Mr Brown had been about to say 'I don't know about that', but he felt rather than saw everybody else in the room staring at him, so he changed his mind.

"Whatever you say, Mary," he replied meekly.

Luckily Paddington arrived downstairs at that point.

"I've finished my postcard to Aunt Lucy," he announced, "so I thought I would go and post it, but I can't find my duffle coat anywhere. I wonder if we ought to ring for the police?"

The Browns exchanged anxious glances.

"I really shouldn't worry, dear," said Mrs Brown. "I'm sure it will turn up. You're too late for the last post anyway."

"You know what I think," said Jonathan, coming to the rescue. "If you're going to be famous, you ought to have a *nom de plume*."

"I've never had one of those before," said Paddington. "It sounds interesting. What is it?"

"It's French for what's known as a 'pen name'," said Judy. "Writers use them when they don't want people to know their real name."

"Film stars do it all the time," agreed Mrs Brown. "Except they call it their 'stage name'. Michael Caine was born Maurice Micklewhite. I heard him talking about it on television only the other day."

"And Fred Astaire started life as Frederick Austerlitz," said Jonathan. "That's a famous French railway station."

"I'm not surprised he changed it," said Paddington. "I wouldn't like to be called Austerlitz."

"In fact," said Mrs Bird, "come to think of it, you have a *nom de plume* already. If you remember, when you arrived over here you had a Peruvian name which you weren't too sure about, so that's how you came to be called Paddington, because that's where Mr and Mrs Brown found you."

"If you're likely to be signing lots of autographs I should change it to Pad," said Jonathan, mindful of how long it took Paddington to write a postcard. "It'll save lots of time."

But Paddington clearly had his mind on other things as he headed towards the kitchen.

"I would rather you didn't go in there…" began Mrs Bird, but she was too late.

"It's all right, Mrs Bird," called Paddington. "Don't worry. I've found my duffle coat. It's underneath the tea towel. I wonder how it got there?"

"There are no flies on Paddington," said Judy.

"That bear's got his head screwed on the right way," agreed Mrs Bird.

"My head's screwed on!" exclaimed Paddington, as he came back into the room. "I didn't know that!"

"There's no need to worry about it, dear," said Mrs Brown. "It won't fall off in a hurry."

"I hope it doesn't fall off at all," said Paddington hotly.

"I might have a nightmare and turn over quickly in my sleep," he added darkly. "I dreamt I was being chased by a bumblebee the other night and I had to run all over the house before it flew out of an open window by mistake."

"Changing the subject," said Jonathan, "we've been wondering, supposing, just supposing the film is very successful and you become famous overnight, you might, well… we might not see quite so much of you again, except on the screen."

"Not see quite so much of me?" exclaimed Paddington in alarm. "I can't picture that…"

"That's part of the trouble, Paddington," said Mrs Brown, voicing the thoughts of the others. "Neither can we."

At which point everyone agreed it was time for bed, although it was safe to say that for once sleep didn't come easily, either that night, or for the next few nights as the tension began to mount.

The worst part was not so much being ignorant of what was going on, but with Paddington leaving early every day in a chauffeur-driven car and not arriving back until late in the evening, much too tired to talk, the house seemed unusually quiet.

It was left to Judy to voice their unspoken thoughts. "I can't help feeling we're being bypassed," she said. "And without so much as a by-your-leave."

"Nonsense!" said Mrs Bird in her down-to-earth manner. "It's Paddington's life. He must do as he thinks fit."

Nevertheless, it was noticeable that she took particular trouble with his marmalade sandwiches before he left home in the mornings, often adding an extra one for good measure.

In the event, although it seemed to take forever, the filming came to an end much sooner than anyone had expected.

Fernando arrived back with Paddington early

one evening, and he was carrying a small parcel.

"*Olè*," he said. "I have everything ona da disc so that you can watch it on your television. I see you have a player."

It took only a moment or two for Jonathan to load it, and as soon as everyone was ready and the curtains were drawn he pressed the button.

Mr Brown nearly leapt out of his seat as the opening shot of their front garden filled the screen, revealing a bare patch of paving overlaid with the titles. "Someone has moved my begonias!" he cried. "What's happened to them?"

"Shhh, Henry," hissed Mrs Brown. "They're back in their proper place now."

"That's me!" exclaimed Paddington excitedly, as the film dissolved into a shot of a green area somewhere in London. The camera zoomed in on a group of some dozen or so hurdles lined up one after the other, and carried on zooming until it reached a familiar figure at the far end.

There was a moment's pause allowing Paddington time to raise his hat to a small group of spectators. Then, as the scene changed to a wide shot, a gun went off, galvanising him into action. From being a small figure in the distance, he ended up some seconds later filling the screen in close-up. Whereupon, breathing heavily, he raised his hat again; this time to camera.

The Browns sat in silence for a moment or two.

"I must say he was going very fast," ventured

Judy. "I see now why they're called 'rushes'."

"I can't wait for the real thing," agreed Jonathan.

Señor Fernando looked put out. "Whata you mean, da real thing?" he demanded. "They are nota da rushes. That is it… the whole caboodle… the finished film."

"We did over thirty retakes," said Paddington. "I lost count in the end."

"Er… I don't wish to sound over-critical," said Mr Brown, "but…"

"You no like?" asked Fernando. "You are upset about your begonias?"

"Well, it's not exactly that," said Mr Brown. "What little we saw is beautifully made, I grant you, but it does seem to me it has what one might call a basic design fault."

"The film? It hasa da basic design fault?" repeated Fernando. "What you mean, *señor*? A basic design fault?"

"Well," said Mr Brown, taking a deep breath. "Shouldn't Paddington be jumping *over* the hurdles rather than going underneath them."

"Ah," exclaimed Fernando. "You English. I knew

when I first set eyes on you, *Señor* Brown, you are a da perfectionist at heart."

"I didn't bang my head once, Mr Brown," said Paddington. "I kept my hat on all the time, just in case."

"Well," said Mr Brown. "It isn't so much that, but I strongly suspect other people may notice it too."

"Just as a matter of interest," said Judy. "What made you choose the hurdles?"

"Mr Gruber told me he was good at them when he was young," said Paddington. "So I thought I might have a go."

"Ask a silly question…" said Jonathan.

"All the same, it does seem a bit of a let down," said Mrs Brown.

"The film is nota for general release," said Fernando.

"Thank goodness for that," murmured Mr Brown.

"It is for the inhabitants of the Home for Retired Bears in Lima," explained Fernando. "Most of them have no idea whata da hurdle race is, let alone set eyes ona da moving picture. Over them… under them… who is to care? It is all the same. And after all, they are paying for it. To them it will be a moment of great excitement that will last for the rest of their lives."

He turned to Mrs Brown.

"*Señora*, you will remember the first time a moving picture was shown in Paris. Those neara da screen ran for cover when a train appeared and headed straight towards them. They thought their end hada da come."

"I'm afraid I don't," said Mrs Brown. "It was before my time."

"1895," said Jonathan knowledgeably. "It was an early Lumière Brothers film."

Fernando looked at him. "You should goa da far," he said.

"What bothers me, Paddington," broke in Mr Brown hastily, "meaning no disrespect, but what made Sunny Climes think you were such an athlete in the first place? I mean, talk about getting hold of the wrong end of the stick, but doing something like a mile and a half in under four minutes beggars belief."

"I meant to tell him, I was in your car at the

time, Mr Brown," said Paddington. "We were going to meet Jonathan at the station. But then I thought you might be in trouble for going so fast, and I didn't want you to be arrested, so I kept it to myself."

"How about the one hundred metres in five seconds?" asked Jonathan.

"If the buns are just out of the oven," said Paddington simply, "you need to do it as fast as you can. Especially if you've only got paws."

"You know something," said Fernando, breaking the silence that followed. "That bear, his head is what you might call screwed on a righta da way. It has been a da pleasure working with him!"

"There you are, Paddington," said Mrs Bird. "I told you so."

"I'm sorry the film isa no longer," said Fernando, "but as you say in your country, 'good things come ina da small parcels'."

"It may be a small film to you," said Mr Brown, "but I must say it's a big relief to all of us."

"I give you the disc asa da present to remember me by," said Fernando.

Brushing aside all offers of refreshment, he left

as smoothly as he had arrived. First he reached for Mrs Bird's hand in order to bestow a kiss, then he bowed to the rest of the family.

Mrs Bird drew the curtains and the Browns gathered by the window to watch as Paddington accompanied Fernando to the gate. They doffed their hats to each other as they said a final goodbye. At which point Fernando presented Paddington with the peacock's feather from his hat, and with a final wave he went on his way.

Paddington responded, and then instead of entering the house by the front door, he disappeared down the side.

"Now where's he going?" said Mr Brown.

"Quick," said Judy. "After him!"

Led by Jonathan, they all rushed out into the back garden through the kitchen door, but Paddington had beaten them to it. He was sitting on one of the stones in his rockery looking up at the sunflowers.

"Well," said Jonathan. "Any more films in the offing?"

"I don't know," said Paddington. "Mr Fernando said I wasn't to ring him, he would ring me."

"But…" began Mr Brown. He was about to say that was what all film producers said when the answer was 'no', but Paddington didn't give him the chance.

"I don't think I would like to be a film star," he said. "I wouldn't want to leave Windsor Gardens. I think it's the nicest place in all the world."

As the Browns gave a collected sigh of relief Mrs Bird reached for her handkerchief. "I do like films that have a happy ending," she said, dabbing at her eyes. "Why don't we go indoors and see yours all over again."

Paddington jumped to his feet. "Let me do it, Mrs Bird," he exclaimed. "Bears are good at pressing buttons."

The Browns exchanged glances. "Goodness knows what we shall see now," said Mr Brown. "You know what Paddington's like with buttons."

Mrs Brown gave his arm a squeeze. "To tell you the truth, Henry," she said. "I'm so relieved I really don't mind what it is."